Rootbound

Rootbound

GRANT BUDAY

ECW PRESS

Copyright © Grant Buday, 2006

Published by ECW PRESS
2120 Queen Street East, Suite 200, Toronto, Ontario, Canada M4E 1E2

All rights reserved. No part of this publication may be reproduced, stored in a retrieval system, or transmitted in any form by any process — electronic, mechanical, photocopying, recording, or otherwise — without the prior written permission of the copyright owners and ECW PRESS.

LIBRARY AND ARCHIVES CANADA CATALOGUING IN PUBLICATION

Buday, Grant, 1956–
Rootbound / Grant Buday.

"a misFit book".
ISBN 1-55022-748-3

1. Title.

PS8553.U444R66 2006   C813'.54   C2006-904115-6

Editor for the press: Michael Holmes / a misFit book
Cover and Text Design: Tania Craan
Cover Art: Bernice Eisenstein
Typesetting: Mary Bowness
Printing: Transcontinental

This book is set in Adobe Garamond

The publication of *Rootbound* has been generously supported by the Canada Council, the Ontario Arts Council, and the Government of Canada through the Book Publishing Industry Development Program.

DISTRIBUTION
CANADA: Jaguar Book Group, 100 Armstrong Ave., Georgetown, ON L7G 5S4

PRINTED AND BOUND IN CANADA

ECW PRESS
ecwpress.com

To my mother and father, master craftsmen

And God said, Let the earth bring forth grass . . .

THEY CROSSED THE YARD IN single file, three silhouettes bent low in the night, the only sound the muted clank of tools in a nylon sports bag. One after the other they descended the cement stairwell as if proceeding into the earth itself en route to some subterranean rendezvous. A twist of a crowbar and the door drifted open. They listened — hearing only their own heartbeats and the rasp of their breath through the itchy wool of their balaclavas. They entered and shut the door.

The leader peeled the mask off his head, exposing a shaved skull and a handlebar moustache of Hungarian rakishness. His taut black T-shirt highlighted a savagely muscular torso. He listened again and the others waited for his signal. None of them had been there before but they all recognized the smell that told them they were in the right place. The others stripped off their balaclavas and grinned the grins of people excited by their work. They knew the pride that came with job satisfaction. One of the thieves was a woman. She shook out the gnarly hair stuck to her face. Like a cavalry officer signalling a charge, the leader motioned them forward, guiding them to a second door which, with another twist of the crowbar and a splintering of wood, popped open. It was as if they'd freed a stellar god, a creature of brilliance, radiant and pure, from its stone prison. They raised their arms to shield their eyes: it wasn't the blaze of an avenging angel, but high-pressure sodium lights in melon-sized bulbs sizzling above a crop of marijuana, as pungent as new piss. Ten tables with twelve plants each, worth sixty thousand dollars. The leader exhaled a satisfied sigh and gazed upon his colleagues. Had he not promised riches? Had he not been true to his word? He reached into the blue hockey bag and handed out the Ray-Bans and pruning scissors. They went to work. Soon their faces were shellacked with sweat in the heat of the 1000-watt lamps. There was no talk, only the snick of the scissors and the rustle of leaves as they cut the thumb-thick stalks. Moving in tandem down each table they harvested the crop, shoving the plants deep into green plastic garbage bags.

Ten minutes and they were done. They looked upon their work and were pleased. They'd left a single lone plant untouched in the middle of the room. "Don't want to discourage him," the leader said in a deep voice that was not without sincerity, for he appreciated the moral dimension in the equation of labour and reward. And with that they fled into the night.

CHAPTER 1

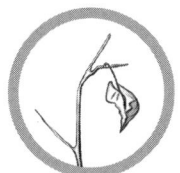

TO CELEBRATE HIS FIFTIETH BIRTHDAY, Willie gave Carmen $150 so she could buy him dinner in the Grouse Nest atop Grouse Mountain, a restaurant accessible only by cable car, unless you preferred an hour's vertical hike and the risk of a coronary with your wine. They both ordered New York steaks, and throughout the meal Carmen repeatedly lay down her knife and fork to better devote herself to the view of Vancouver. Willie was glad she was enjoying it, and when she made appreciative noises he made them too, even though he thought the city looked as if it had been poured from a trash bin, spilling off the land and into the lead-grey sea. The place looked like so much rubble, and it lay beneath a pall of fumes that suggested a smouldering bog.

"The air would be cleaner in a smaller town," he suggested, trying to kindle Carmen's interest in getting away from Vancouver and scouting the interior for an orchard. Willie's orchard fantasy involved a valley sweetened by a river, and row after row of apple trees laden with fruit. Reaching across the bleached tablecloth he took Carmen's hand. "Close your eyes."

She liked that. Her smile widened and her dimples deepened. She had large grey eyes, perfect teeth, auburn hair, and a moonlight complexion that, depending upon her mood, could either lose its glow and look like lard, or, thanks to a carafe of house red, appear warm and flushed. Her most remarkable feature was her forehead, so wide and high that Willie couldn't help but picture the throbbing machinery of her brain.

Willie's voice became sensuous and coaxing. "It's spring. The orchard is in flower. Smell." He inhaled. "Hundreds of trees, millions of blossoms. Now it's summer. The evening sunlight angling in. It's hot. The trees are thick with fruit. Kings, Braeburns, Jonagolds. . . ." Carmen's breathing deepened as if the very names were getting her excited. Willie knew she was indulging him. For her, apples meant the Safeway produce aisle.

"I love it," she lied.

"I'm glad."

But that was only part of the fantasy. Along with the orchard would be the house Willie would build: hardwood floors, beamed ceilings, river-rock fireplace, alcoves, sunroom, wraparound porch, cedar-shake roof, maybe a gazebo.

"We can do it," said Carmen, drunk.

As well as celebrating his birthday, they were celebrating

the crop, and the fact that Willie had promised to buy her a vintage robin's egg blue BMW 321i convertible that was sitting in a lot across town. She had it all picked out to match her self-image: the serious artist, scarf tied pirate style around her head, the car's stereo pumping the *Carmina Burana* as the sunshine followed her like a spotlight.

After dinner they strolled arm in arm along the restaurant's alpine paths lined with daffodils. It was nearly eight o'clock on a spring evening and the lingering daylight was like land reclaimed from the sea. This morning the newspaper had gloatingly run a photo of local plum blossoms alongside a shot of Torontonians digging their cars out of snow. Carmen clung to Willie's arm and rested her head on his shoulder. Heat rushed to his groin as if a bulb had gone on in his new khakis.

"I want to do a nude of you," she whispered. "You've got such a great back."

Him? Flattered, Willie tried visualizing his back. V-shaped? Not really. Broad-shouldered? No. More of a melting candle.

They lived in the far reaches of the East End, an area unburdened by charm, notable only for that drabbest of construction, The Vancouver Special, which was less a home than a container, two crates one atop the other with holes punched at either end, the sort of thing in which a boy might keep hamsters. The Vancouver Special was utilitarian. No fuss, no muss, no extras, with gravel instead of a front lawn. Its single concession to style was the pair of cement lions, often mistaken for dogs, flanking the cheap wrought iron gate.

Willie and Carmen did not live in a Vancouver Special, they occupied a two-floor, two-bedroom house circa 1950. On this night of nights, his fiftieth birthday, his Big Five Oh, Willie bumped slowly down the alley in the van and pulled into the carport and switched off the ignition. Before getting out, they leaned toward each other and kissed beneath the Attar of Rose deodorizer dangling like mistletoe from the rear-view mirror. Carmen tasted of wine and Nicorettes. He was proud of her for quitting. She'd gone two weeks and was feeling confident. Her lips were soft and, if not exactly sweet, they were willing. They kissed and murmured *I love you* and then crossed the lawn with their arms around each other. The back porch light glinted on the stucco. Willie liked stucco, bits of brown and green glass embedded in masonry, cost-effective and yet attractive, always there to reflect even the briefest flash of sun.

While Carmen showered, Willie popped downstairs to say goodnight to his babies.

When he discovered what had happened, he dropped to his knees and raised his hands in a state of spiritual agony. His plants, his girls, the tender creatures he'd nurtured from seedlings, gone. Under the burning blaze of the lights, all that remained were their bleeding stumps, even as the pump continued sending water through the tubes that fed each pot — clay balls holding the roots that had been rendered useless by the brutal amputations.

And there was the single plant that had been spared, a solitary survivor of slaughter, a lone witness to events terrible to behold, not just a message but a gesture of malicious glee. They were laughing at him.

Carmen came down the steps, jiggly and pink and naked beneath her white terrycloth bathrobe with its gold trim, crooning a melodious "Willie . . ." for it was understood that a back rub and sex were to complete this evening of evenings.

He turned and watched her take it all in, watched the transformation of her mind and her mood, her expression plunging from one of sensual anticipation to confusion, and, finally, terror. Carmen began to moan and tremble as if in the throes of a palsy. She fell against the washing machine and her tiger's eye ring tapped a spastic sos on the metal.

"Carmen —"

She reached out beseechingly, the robe falling from her shoulder revealing a Rembrandt breast. "What if we'd've been here?"

Willie saw the nightmare trampling Carmen's mind. Humiliation, blood, rape. He caught her hands and held them. He spoke in a tone of reasonableness and calm. "Take it easy. Relax. They knew we were out." He immediately saw his error. "Carmen . . . Carmen . . ."

"They were watching? We're being watched!" Her eyes rolled like a cow comprehending all too late what those men in the black rubber aprons intended to do with their cleavers.

Willie tried to embrace her but she backed away, her fingers in her mouth, and fled upstairs.

❧

Willie had raised his pot plants from cuttings. They were his children and their optimism had won his heart. He nurtured them through their phases and maladies, their blights and rusts and scabs, until the seedlings were no longer seedlings but hardy young plants taking their place in the world. One hundred and twenty plants that would stand over a metre high.

He'd spent hours each day with them, the radio tuned to AM 600, waxing nostalgic to Dionne Warwick, Petula Clark, and Herb Alpert, music that had filled his childhood. He loved the feel of their leaves, as coarse as a cat's tongue, against his cheek. He inhaled their tart spice, admired them in their clean-limbed youth and then, later, in their lush green maturity. When he altered the light to simulate autumn and coax them into bud, the relationship evolved into a new seriousness. Bud meant money. His beauties were becoming a cash crop. As he talked to them his voice took on a huskier tone. When the branches bent under the weight of bud, Willie became fearful and excited, for his little ladies were pregnant and glistening with sugary resin. Yet with this stage came guilt. They were destined for the fires of reefers and water pipes and oven-baked brownies. Still, wasn't that marijuana's *raison d'etre* — to entrance the smoker, to enhance their life, to heighten and brighten and delight, to re-enchant food and music and the toker's every sense? Of course. But it was his first crop, and like any first-time parent he'd had no way of comprehending the depth of the bond. He became maudlin and philosophical, talking to the plants in ways he never did to people, of life, of death, of *what-it-all-meant*, and offering thanks for what they were giving him, not just money, but a sense of pride and accomplishment, and most of all the relationship, yes, the relationship, the chance to know them, the honour of loving them.

And then they were kidnapped. He never even got a change to say goodbye.

❧

Over the following months Willie mourned. He gazed longingly at the photographs he'd taken and recalled individual plants, the quirk of a stalk or leaf, its position at the edge or middle of the crop. But he also grew determined. He shored up his defences. He installed motion detectors, a steel-framed door and crossbar, bolted iron grilles over all the windows and parked blocks away whenever he visited hydroponics shops. Rarely did he go to the same shop twice. Never would it happen again.

Carmen went back to smoking cigarettes and her voice grew hoarse. "Go back into construction."

"With *my* back?"

"Don't bend over. Don't lift anything. Hire grunts. Delegate."

Having once owned a company called Top Floor Construction, Willie could drive around Vancouver and point to the houses — the homes — he'd built, having overseen seventy-three of them from the foundation on up. Over the years he'd become intimate with every step of the process. He could get in there and frame, roof, paint, tile, lay a floor, install a window, build kitchen cabinets, plumb, and wire. He loved the scent of fir and cedar, and nothing could be more beautiful than autumn sunlight gleaming in a rubylike drop of sap beading from a two-by-four. He'd been happy in his work; he could say, with pride: I'm a builder. But when he hit the age of forty his back had said something else: No more. It made its position known via chronic pains and spasms. He hobbled around the site leaning on a cane and every winter it got worse, so that by the time he was forty-five his back was locked up like a rusted vise. Then his knees and his shoulders went, followed by numbness in his hands. In the middle of the night he'd get up and pee all the colours of the rainbow. Eventually his entire body throbbed like a toothache.

CHAPTER 2

GETTING ROBBED HAD MADE for a discouraging start, but for Willie LeMat discouragement was as close as the nearest mirror. Not that he was ugly; he just wasn't handsome. Despite all the toothpaste, baking soda, mouthwash, Pearl Drops, bleaches and whiteners, his teeth continued to go grey as steadily as his hair, which, once thick and brown and curly, had receded like a tide that would never return. Soulful eyes would have compensated for his lumpy nose and thin lips, but his eyes were not soulful — not according to his mother, who, from as far back as Willie could remember, had impressed upon him the fact that he had his father's eyes, which, she said, looked like gallstones. No idea what gallstones were much less what they looked like, Willie had found the word in the dictionary:

a small hard concretion of cholesterol, bile pigments, and lime salts formed in the gall bladder or its ducts. Of course, the fact that his father had abandoned them might have had something to do with Mrs. LeMat's opinion. Willie's mother had died before meeting Carmen, which was unfortunate because Carmen would have filled the awkward silences that had always burdened the LeMat household.

Carmen liked to talk. Willie never confronted her with his suspicion that her habit of talking to strangers in lineups and elevators and restaurants had been the leak that caused the rip-off. What could that achieve? Honesty was a noble thing in its way, yet in Willie's experience honesty was also something to be wary of, especially in a relationship, because once said some things could never be unsaid. Not that he lied or cheated or deceived — never once had he played around on Carmen, and he'd certainly never played around on Mercedes — yet he believed books promoting honesty in relationships were naive, written by people who'd never been married, or who were divorced and secretly wanted to see everyone else divorced as well.

One thing was certain though: there had been a leak. The timing of the rip-off had been too lucky for an accident. The only way the timing could have been better was if they'd come seventy-two hours later and the crop had been trimmed and bagged and waiting to be carried off. Willie's only satisfaction — and it was a small one — was in knowing the bastards would have to trim a limp crop, which was like untying knots in wet shoelaces while wearing oven mitts. But who blabbed? Angela at some drunken university party? It'd be easy to go too far and say too much about Daddy the dope grower. Unless, as he often feared, she was humiliated by him and avoided all mention of him. Besides, she went to school in Seattle, so the thieves would have had a border to cross. He was stymied. Carmen, Angela, Juliet, Rollo. . . . There they were, his entire world, each one financially dependent on him: a dysfunctional extended family of which he was the hub.

Carmen was not the only one who had been traumatized by the robbery. Even now, months later, Willie would wake with a pounding heart from nightmare visions of bat-wielding intruders. It was not in the nature of his relationship with Carmen to confide his fears. He'd learned early that such confessions caused her to frown and withdraw as if she'd been betrayed, as if Willie were flawed goods. So he remained adamantly optimistic and did the only thing he could, which was to get back in the saddle and start another crop. He went through the entire process all over, nurturing the seedlings, replanting them, monitoring the phosphorus and the nutrients and the water temperature, altering the lights to simulate autumn, and finally bringing them to bud. It had taken three months, but he'd done it; he had a new crop, and once again the basement was a tropical vale of glorious green. He loved these plants all the more because he knew how easily they could be taken away, and he vowed to protect them.

Today they were finishing up the harvest. This was it. He and Carmen had spent the last three days cutting down the plants and trimming off the fan leaves and the extraneous foliage. They did not apologize to the plants, no sir, they congratulated each and every one of them as if it were their graduation, their coming-of-age ceremony. There was much to celebrate. Willie was anticipating a twenty-five pound crop, which, even allowing for recent price fluctuations, would earn him close to sixty thousand dollars. By any measurement it should have been a day of joy, a triumphant return, a testament to the perseverance of Willie LeMat, Marijuana Mogul.

"Don't be stupid, Willie. They're watching." All day Carmen had been battering him with her sheet-metal voice. "I'm telling you. Those guys, the ones who robbed us, they're out there. They're watching." When Willie said nothing, she shook her head and looked forlorn, as if such foresight, such knowledge of the inevitable, was a burden too weighty to bear.

Willie had begun to suspect that his beloved Carmen hoped something would go wrong just to prove herself right. He knew that it was more than fear; she was feeling helpless, and her inability to influence him frustrated her. But a barnacle-like obstinacy was all he had. And anyway he'd been doing a little watching for himself, keeping his eye out for suspicious activity, and he was feeling confident that they were okay. After all, the poachers couldn't possibly assume they could just waltz on in a second time. They'd have to anticipate resistance, barriers, alarms, booby traps, something. "It's fine," he assured her. And to show how fine it was, he switched on the radio in time to catch Herb Alpert with his quick-tapping trumpet. Willie casually raised the volume in hopes that it would speed Carmen up, for despite her skill with a pen and brush, she was a slow and clumsy trimmer. Just the tips of the leaves, he kept reminding her, wincing as she gouged and mutilated yet another bud.

"San Miguel de Allende," she said. "I was there in the '80s.

There's lots of foreigners. All we have to do is pack up and go. The tropics, Willie. I could teach art classes. I could paint. I need some colour. I'm in a rut. It'd be good for me — for us. I'd support us. You wouldn't even have to work. Think of it. You could get a Panama hat; you'd look good in a Panama hat." She tipped her head to one side for a better angle. "Yeah. And a cigar. A *cigarillo*. A long slim one."

"What, like Ricardo Montalban?"

She was disgusted. "No. Not like Ricardo Montalban. Like *Pancho Villa*."

"Pancho Villa?" He could never tell when she was serious or joking because he suspected that she couldn't tell either. She might have said it off the top of her head and liked the sound of it so decided to believe it. Like Frida Kahlo's eyebrows. For a while she'd been obsessed with the way Frida Kahlo's eyebrows met and formed a dark bar. Carmen had taken an eyebrow pencil and joined up her own, insisting it strengthened her face. It certainly made people look twice, which she liked. She carried herself differently, taller, more confident, and around the house had even toyed with a Mexican accent. It evolved into a game, she calling him *Weelee* and he calling her *Carmelita*, both of them growing adventurous and plunging recklessly into the blind alleys of Spanish sentences that they had no idea how to finish, except on the bed or couch making love. That lasted a month. He didn't know why she stopped. When he'd asked her, she'd shrugged as if she'd forgotten the entire episode. He feared he could never touch bottom with Carmen, that he was always afloat and uncertain.

At the moment, they were seated on opposite sides of a

ping-pong table heaped with pot plants, trimming the last few stalks. It was late afternoon, and in an hour Rollo and Juliet would arrive to celebrate. Willie had bought steaks and wine and beer. He watched as Carmen stabbed and hacked at a fist-sized bud. A lousy trimmer. He'd like to go back over the entire crop but that'd take forever. They needed to make the sale and get some money. He had no doubt she was sincere in her resolve to teach art classes and support them in this San Miguel de Allende. Nor did he doubt that if they actually went there, her resolve would be replaced by a new and equally sincere one that didn't involve her teaching and supporting them. Instead of asking her what he would do with all his leisure time in Mexico, he restated the facts. "The door is reinforced. The windows are reinforced. We're safe. Nothing's happened and nothing's going to happen."

"Nothing's happened because they're waiting for the right time. I can *feel* it."

What could he say to that? Predatory assaults on grow-ops had become a sub-trade of the marijuana industry. Opportunistic vultures too lazy and dull-witted to grow their own were often ballsy enough to bust in your door. You just had to learn to live with it and take precautions.

Suddenly frustrated with Herb Alpert, Carmen shoved the radio off the table into the cardboard Smirnoff box full of bud where Herb continued to play "Tijuana Taxi." She hugged herself as if chilled, and looked around, her tortured gaze travelling the cement walls and open-joisted ceiling. "You said we'd get sixty maybe seventy grand. We could last years on that in Mexico."

"We'd last two, tops. Then what?"

"I don't want to die, Willie."

He stared at her in exhaustion and disbelief.

Carmen was insulted. "What if they're waiting outside tonight?"

"There's a motion detector."

"What if someone smells something and calls the cops?"

Willie pointed to the keg-sized carbon filter he'd installed in place of the ozone generator to mask the unmistakable stink of pot. He'd pointed it out a hundred times. She'd been there when he bought it and she'd watched him install it, and yet she didn't seem to trust it; to her it was just some flimsy metal contraption.

A veil of concern darkening her eyes, Carmen now reached across and pressed his hand. "I don't want you to go to jail, Willie. The very thought of you in jail . . ." Her voice thickened with the onset of tears.

He felt the strange sensation of her fingers through the surgical gloves. "I'm not going to jail."

"If this was the States you'd get ten years."

Willie didn't know what he'd get in the States, but what he did know was that he had a clean record, so up here in Beautiful British Columbia, jail was highly unlikely, no, impossible.

"A reasonable adult would be exploring alternative career paths, Willie. Like school. You want to go back to school, fine, do it, I'm behind you."

"I'm fifty."

"Exactly." She gestured around at the absurdity of a grow-op. "A bit old for this, don't you think?"

Stung, Willie said nothing.

"Look. It was a lark. It was fun. I admit it. I was having a great time; you were having a great time. But we were naive. We got burned, Willie, we got *burned*. This is crime, remember how we talked about it being crime? Well, it is, and someone has our number. Someone bad. Someone violent."

Willie grasped her point and largely agreed with it. He endured the same fears she did; nonetheless he shook his head. "We need to hang in and grow at least eight more crops. That'll get us half a million. It won't take long. A couple of years." When he saw the horror in her eyes at the notion of two more years of dope-growing he talked faster, with the urgency of a preacher. "Then we're free. We're done. We can retire. If we're smart we can live off that for the rest of our lives! Think of it, Carmen."

She didn't want to think of it. She threw down the branch she was trimming as well as the sixty-dollar pair of Japanese-crafted grapevine scissors, and sat with her arms crossed and her lips compressed into a thin line.

Willie patiently picked up her branch and finished it properly, snipping away the fan leaves as well as the tips of the smaller leaves — the honey leaves — around the glistening buds. "We'll talk about it after the crop. It's all theory until the crop's sold and we have cash in hand. We can't even consider Mexico — or anything else — until we sell the stuff."

Eyes hard as drill bits, she stared, determined to mark this moment and hold him to his words. "Fine."

"We move the crop and we'll be sitting on sixty grand. We will then be in a position to exercise options." He liked the word "options" because it implied freedom. Taking a moment to admire the fist-sized buds on the foot-long branch, he placed it gently, as if fearful of bruising it, in the cardboard box along with the others and retrieved the radio and set it back on the table. Herb had been replaced by Tony Bennett singing about his heart in San Francisco. Another song from Willie's youth. Willie picked up the branch he'd been working on and resumed snipping the foliage. "Isn't this a beauty?"

He knew that the way he fawned over the plants made Carmen jealous, but he couldn't help himself, he loved them. Willie would have been flattered if Carmen would paint them, a bouquet of marijuana with a bowl of apples and maybe a brace of pheasant or a rabbit. He wanted her to appreciate the accomplishment of the crop, to marvel at the heft of the forearm-sized branch of bud he was trimming, which, depending on its density, was worth close to a thousand dollars. No rare orchid gathered from the mossy green depths of the old growth forest was more special to Willie.

"Just hang in for this last bit." He grinned in an overearnest attempt to infuse her with enthusiasm. He sincerely believed, or at least hoped, that with a few successful crops behind them her enthusiasm would be rekindled. Yet all this earned him was a harsh exhalation from Carmen's nose as if she were trying to expel an insect. She stood and stripped off her surgical gloves, let them dangle and drop as if they were used condoms, and turned without a word and went upstairs.

Willie took the freshly barbered buds into the drying room and began hooking the branches upside down on the wires running along the rafters. The entire ceiling was thick with dangling green bud: a hanging garden of marijuana. He adjusted the spacing and re-angled the electric fans so the crop would dry evenly. It was a good crop. The particular strain he grew was known as "green fields," offering a clean and functional high, not the knock-down drag-out skunk weed that left you gibbering or comatose. When he returned to the trimming table he spotted Carmen's gloves in a heap, the fingertips crusted in a thick green resin. "That's hash, you know," he said out loud. "All you have to do is scrape it off and press it." He went through the garbage collecting all the surgical gloves they'd used, snipped off the resin-rich fingertips, and put them in a Ziploc baggie. If he collected enough resin he could press hash and design his own label to stamp into the bricks. *LeMat green*. Someday it might make it into the lexicon alongside blond Leb and Nepalese temple balls. In its own small way a touch of immortality. He scraped the pot resin from both pairs of trimming scissors then rubbed the blades with alcohol and then hung them on their nail. Finally, he checked the basement door, a metal door-and-frame with a two-by-ten cross bar. Solid. You could run a tank against it and it would hold.

CHAPTER 3

WILLIE WAS STILL IN THE BASEMENT cleaning up when he heard footsteps on the backstairs. That would be Rollo. Willie peeled off his gloves, dusted the leaves from his sweatshirt, admired his crop one last time, and headed on up to the kitchen, eager for Rollo to see the crop and the festivities to begin. As soon as he saw Rollo's face, however, he knew there was trouble.

Rollo opened his arms in an apologetic shrug. "Buddy. Hey. Gotta raise the rent."

"To what?"

"Three."

"*Three thousand a month?*"

Rollo did his best to appear the victim, difficult given he was looking so richly tanned from four weeks in Puerto Vallarta

— PV — and was sipping one of Willie's beers. He was already charging twenty-five hundred a month rent, five hundred more than the house was worth. Still, he did a good job of looking wronged, as if he wasn't to blame but *them*, those evil forces Out There. If it was up to Rollo he'd let Willie and Carmen live here free, perhaps even pay them to take care of the place which was, after all, his family home, the place he'd grown up in, the house in which he had learned to walk and talk and play the upright bass.

Like Willie, Rollo was fifty years old, but unlike Willie he was trying to look thirty. He combed his rusty hair forward to cover the increasing acreage of exposed scalp, and he was sporting a soul patch, a disconcertingly pubic-looking tuft of dampish hair beneath his lower lip. He wore a tight black T-shirt with a gold Paper Mate hooked over the collar as if he anticipated autograph seekers. Black suede shoes with tan laces and black jeans completed the ensemble. This was his Chicago Jazz look. For besides being a carpet layer, pot farmer and all around bum wart, he was a musician, and owned various electric bass guitars as well as uprights including an Immanuel Shpak vox — Buchresti with smile frets and reindeer-gut strings. He'd recently cut a CD, *Rollo Does Ron*, a seventy-seven minute bass solo inspired by the work of Rollo's idol, the legendary Ron Carter. Rollo had financed it himself, and never went anywhere without half a dozen copies, passing them out to the ladies like business cards. At five-foot-four, he was not exactly the long lean soul brother of his fantasies, yet when he toked he was transformed into his real self, his best self, his ideal Rollo, fascinating to women and fearsome to men, a spliff-city groove-meister all of six-foot-three, the toast of the jazz cellars up and down the coast from Vancouver to L.A. Whatever else could be said about Rollo, his love of jazz was sincere, dating from his discovery — at the age of thirteen — of an album called *Slightly Latin* by Rahsaan Roland Kirk in the local library. The album cover was soft and round-cornered with handling, the disk itself scratchy with years of abuse on blunt-needled hi-fis. But the music . . . Whimsical, swift, melodious. Kirk often played three saxophones at once. Rollo was inspired and in love and his thirteen-year-old life would never be the same. Of course he stole the album, sprinting out of the library with it under his coat one winter afternoon, and never showed his face there again. Unfortunately, his early efforts at the saxophone were disheartening. His lips hurt and he sounded like a tortured goose, and then there was the business of all the saliva. He looked around; drums were too bulky and expensive, so he finally settled on the bass, first the guitar and then the upright. His callused fingertips were now as hard as dimes and his hands suggestively large.

"I thought you were going to help us out with the trimming?" said Willie.

Rollo dismissed him with a wave, meaning, *you wouldn't believe what I've been through today*. Willie didn't ask for details because he didn't care. It was always bad news with Rollo. If he wasn't jacking the rent he was trafficking in rumours that the cops were slamming growers, or that the pot market was weak so Willie's dope wasn't worth as much, or that Willie's dope just wasn't all that good, and that Willie didn't look all that good either. If nothing else, Rollo would make a point of using the toilet and intentionally forget to flush, though he always had a few complimentary words for Carmen's art, which hung in the living room, the dining room, the kitchen and the hall as well as the bathroom. He would often emerge from the can doing up his zipper and remarking on Carmen's eyes or lips or hair, and Willie would be obliged to wonder just what Rollo had been up to in there.

Willie opened the fridge and got a beer. "Carmen and I spent the last three days trimming."

This obsession with perfectly trimmed pot baffled Rollo, who merely tore the leaves barehanded from his own crop when it came time to harvest.

Rollo said, "Man, give your head a shake. I could've trimmed that whole crop in an hour. Most bozos don't care if there's a few leaves. Once the shit dries it all shrivels up and they can't tell anyhow. All that with the Japanese scissors and the snip-snip-snip." Rollo waved as if batting a fly. He raised his voice now, making it carry, as if he wanted Carmen, who was down the hall in the bedroom getting changed, to hear him speaking in the voice of wisdom. "You gotta get realistic, man. Cut your labour costs. Prioritize. First things first. Step one, step two."

"Rollo, I'm not deaf. I'm right here."

"All I'm saying is take care of essentials — your landlord, *me*. Got another beer in there?"

Willie did not begrudge sharing his beer, but he did expect the superior quality of his imported Czech beer — Pilzn Urquell — to be appreciated, and in Rollo's case that was doubtful. On his own Rollo drank Budweiser, which was like preferring wieners to Parma ham. Willie got Rollo another bottle of beer and sat down. Between them lay the kitchen-table clutter of newspapers, plates, crossword puzzles, and a milk pitcher in the shape of a jersey cow. On the wall hung a boldly crosshatched triptych in pen and ink on heavy cotton stock. Inside their frames, three bold and confident Carmens gazed out, their eyes inducing the unsettling illusion of following you wherever you moved.

"You'll get paid when I get paid," said Willie.

"So pack the shit up and I'll make the call." Rollo had the connection in Seattle, a guy named Dwayne who would come up to the border and meet the mule who would hike the pot across in a backpack. The mule was also Rollo's connection, a kid named Lars who Willie had never met and who probably wasn't even called Lars. Willie would have to give Lars — via Rollo — a thousand dollars for the hundred-yard nature stroll through the scrub, plus a hundred per pound to Rollo as his commission. Once the dope was in Dwayne's hands they'd rendezvous with him at a yet-to-be-specified location and get the cash — all in all, a tenuous arrangement that worried Willie.

"It won't be dry for three days."

"*Three?* You don't need to dry the shit three days. Two, max. You dry it three days you'll lose a thousand bucks of water weight."

"I'm taking it down to seventeen percent."

Rollo began to choke. His feet danced beneath the table as if the floor was on fire. He pointed at Willie and looked around for someone to please talk sense to this guy. "Jesus, man. Twenty's fine."

"It'll get mouldy."

"Earth to Willie, Earth to Willie. Motherfuckin' mould doesn't motherfuckin' matter. There's nothing wrong with mould. Probably makes the shit stronger!"

But Willie refused to sell mouldy pot. Mould looked bad, and he was trying to establish a solid bond with reliable distributors and provide good product for loyal customers. He took pride in perfecting his system; it was the only way he could work. He grew Triple A dope. No, his was the grass of the connoisseur, the thinking man's marijuana, the champagne of smoke, with a taste as rich and complex as Turkish gold leaf. He intended to take it to the Marijuana Olympics in Amsterdam, where even the most obscure grower could go for gold and become a legend.

"I need that money, man." Rollo was shaking his head and staring at the gouged Formica tabletop as if the situation was beyond his control and he might have to do what he might have to do, and who knew what that might have to be?

Willie wondered if Rollo had been the leak. After all, a few beers in him and he'd natter to anyone because of a pathological need to impress. Willie could see him making the moves on some aging lounge queen still trying to look like Stevie Nicks, dropping hints about his dope-growing prowess, which would get passed on to her Angel-associate brother or boyfriend and, one, two, three, Rollo got followed around for a few days during which time he popped in on Willie, and boom the crop was gone.

"I haven't got it."

"You gotta get it."

Willie weighed the tone of voice. He was no fighter, and he knew that you had to be careful of little guys like Rollo, who, if it came down to it, would dig and gouge and bite and spit and scratch. But oh, how Willie would relish the feel of his hands gripping Rollo's throat. Willie wanted to ask: Why now, man? Why grind me now of all times? But he didn't ask because he knew why now. It didn't take an accountant to sort out Rollo's numbers, what he earned and how much he owed, to see that he was living beyond his means. "You just want me to pay for your Mexican holiday, man."

The remark rocked Rollo back into his chair as if he'd been butted in the chest. Unable to breathe, his eyes grew wide and wet with the pain of betrayal and insult.

For a moment Willie was almost moved to apologize but he didn't, he'd said what he'd said and he refused to wilt.

"That crop you lost?" said Rollo. "That was my loss too, you know."

Willie hated confrontation and the tension tightening the air made him dizzy, but he held on. "You lost your commission. Well, I hardly think that's equal to what I lost."

Rollo counted on his fingers. "I bailed you out when you were down. I offered you this house. A safe landlord. And — let me finish — I taught you. I took you under my wing, like an apprentice, a protégé, and taught you everything I know, all the skills I had to learn the hard way — on my own — by trial and error. So why shouldn't I get a commission?"

"I'm not saying you shouldn't get a commission, I'm saying this is a bad time to grind me for more money. It's not even a year and you're already raising the rent!"

Carmen entered the kitchen and opened the fridge for the gala keg of Chablis. Her arrival caused Rollo embarrassment and he immediately discovered a new tone of reasonableness. "We're in this together," he said, as if it were Willie, not him, who was causing dissention.

Carmen brushed at her hair with her fingers to reassure herself that it covered the wide white wall of her forehead with its two bumps. Willie suspected that her Frida Kahlo uni-brow period had been an attempt to divert attention from her forehead. Her forehead put one in mind of a dolphin forebrain bulging with mysterious mental power, a brain capable of painting and drawing with undeniable skill though incapable of comprehending the need to knuckle down and help trim the pot crop. When her hair was wet from the shower and clung to her skull, she could be eerie looking. Now she was wearing a pair of red and grey striped drawstring pants from Ecuador and a black T-shirt with the image of a coiled grey cat taken from an ancient Turkish stone rubbing. In order to hide her forehead, she wore her hair so that it hung like two obscuring curtains.

Holding a green plastic tumbler of wine, she said, "This place is dangerous, Rollo. We're at risk." Rollo began to talk but Carmen cut him off. She could do that, she was female, and any female who wasn't a one-legged leper was Rollo's master. "Willie has been working like a horse, Rollo. Like a horse. You're getting rich off his back." This was too much for Rollo who again tried to speak and again was cut off. Carmen went to Willie and put her arm around his shoulders and gave him a hug as if he were but a poor sharecropper. "A landlord should provide a secure dwelling," she said, as if quoting the Renter's Act.

Rollo glanced at Willie, suspecting a conspiracy against him, their best friend. "Hey, I grew up here. Never got B&E'd once."

Carmen's voice thickened with sarcasm. She cocked her hip and thrust her jaw. "Oh, you mean it's *our* fault? Now I understand!" She put her hand to forehead and turned to Willie. "Willie? Did you know it was our fault? Gee. I guess we should apologize then, huh. I mean, for getting Rollo's house broken into and all."

Rollo, chastised, dialled his beer bottle one way and then the other and waited for her to finish. His ears were throbbing the colour of cranberries. "All I'm saying —"

"All you're saying? What? What are you saying?" demanded Carmen. "Tell me what you're saying. Come on, Rollo. Tell us."

Rollo looked pleadingly at her, as if to say he was but a short, balding man who wanted nothing more than to sit in his room and play his bass, expressing the humble rhythms pulsing through his black-ivory soul. After all he'd done for them, why oh why was this harpy harassing him?

CHAPTER 4

IN THE FLAT HARD SILENCE following Carmen's outburst, footsteps came thumping up the backstairs. Their manner and tone signalled Willie that something was horribly wrong even before his daughter Angela appeared on the porch accompanied by a clean-cut young man who looked like a member of a Christian cult. Angela ignored Carmen and glared at Rollo, who, already shrivelled as a salted slug, shrank even further; finally she looked to her father. Every look they exchanged was a complex knot of guilt and defiance, lament and recrimination.

Willie tried sounding delighted even though he hadn't been expecting her, knowing her mixed attitude toward him, her hatred of Carmen, and her disdain of the grow-op. "Hey! Here she is."

Angela said a furious nothing.

Willie still had trouble believing that his little Angela was a twenty-four-year-old woman. She was what her grandmother Juliet termed, in a charitable choice of words, "plain." In fact Angela was flat-chested, thin-hipped, mousy-haired, and her oatmeal complexion still erupted with acne. Her eyes were the one thing she'd inherited from her mother — big and blue and flecked with gold; and when they weren't bitter they had a faraway quality that could make Willie ache. She'd bounced back and forth between Willie and Mercedes in the years since the divorce. Being there for her was not the issue; the problem was that Willie was *too* there, in her genes, her body, her face. Every time she looked in the mirror she saw her father.

Willie gave her money, bought her Walkmans and Discmans and stereos and TVs, anything to maintain some sort of relationship. As she got older, he suspected she thought she was doing him a favour by accepting his favours. It was the sort of logic she specialized in. On the rare occasions when he withheld she became agitated, and their relationship became chesslike and aggressive, and her final move was always to simply withdraw. Bye-bye. He couldn't bear that. He'd paid her room and board and tuition when she'd moved to Toronto to study documentary filmmaking. He'd paid for music lessons when she wanted to study Celtic harp. He'd paid for university when she'd wanted to teach. He'd paid for technical school when she wanted to be a surveyor. He'd paid for university again when she wanted to study Mandarin. Last year he'd financed her trip through Asia, from which she'd returned not only a Buddhist but three months pregnant by a Burmese monk named "U." She'd been adamant that she was having the baby and would raise it herself, with or without Willie's financial help or moral approval. With pregnancy, she became an initiate in the Great Mystery of the Feminine, something she told him he could never comprehend. He didn't dare deny it. He applauded her principles and at the same feared for her future. He wanted to plead with her not to waste her precious youth in the glorified misery of single parenthood. Time's too short, he wanted to tell her, and there are no prizes for pain. What an expression of patience she gave him whenever he tried saying these things, what a look of infinite sagacity she offered him, as if she were the wise mother and he the naive son. Weeks after arriving home she miscarried, and Willie's guilt intensified due to his secret relief.

The relief did not last long, as she soon enrolled in something called Antioch University down across the line in Seattle — which was no disaster — but she promptly became involved with one of her profs — which was no disaster either, really, except that he was sixty-one years old and had been married four times and had grandchildren Angela's age. His name was Gabriel Irons and they'd been together six months now, so Willie had accepted that the affair had passed the stage of a filthy little fling with a dirty old man and was a genuine relationship, of sorts. Willie had yet to meet the bastard, which worried him, but it was also typical of Angela to withhold. Maybe she was simply going to ride this Gabriel to the grave and walk away with half his estate in American dollars. It was what her mother would have advised.

Now Angela stood on the porch with a young man who

looked like a Bible seller, a curious choice of creature to bring to her father's pot-trimming barbecue. Angela had shaved her head while in Asia, and her hair was now about three inches long, matted and shapeless and intentionally uncombed. In the moment before Willie opened the screen door he experienced various emotions: joy that she'd found someone who looked half decent, dismay at his own conservative leanings, and suspicion about what the guy was up to with his little girl, the daughter to whom he'd read *Curious George*.

When Willie opened the screen door, Angela said, "Don't freak out."

Willie's thoughts reeled. AIDS? Cancer? Pregnancy again? Or had they run off and eloped? He glanced at the guy who was lingering as far away as possible on the porch as if wary, or was it disdainful, of meeting Willie? Did he know what Willie was doing in the basement? Did he smell anything? Even with the crop harvested and the carbon filter booming there was always a risk of smell. He leaned out the door and casually inhaled, testing the air. No, no smell. But a movement caught his eye down to the right. Juliet came around the corner and halted, seeing the threesome on the porch. Juliet was a classic, tall, sixty, with dreadlocked blonde hair weaved with blue glass beads. She had a straight nose and white teeth and ripe lips. There was a faint yellowing about her eyes though, despite regular applications of cucumber slices, and no amount of Mexican aloes and Egyptian unguents could mask the deepening seams in her complexion.

"Hi, Grandma," said Angela.

"Hi, baby. Who's your cute friend?"

Angela shot her a grimace.

Juliet shot one right back as she came on up the steps. Separated by nearly forty years, they seemed to have circled around and met on the far side of the same track as equals, capable of arguing and giggling and confiding. Perhaps it also had to do with the levelling facts of Angela's plain face and Juliet's fading looks, which meant they were each fighting battles they could never win. Willie checked the neighbouring houses for anyone who might be watching, but heard only clanging from inside Ed's Winnebago. Juliet stepped into the kitchen while Willie stayed outside with Angela and the stranger.

"This is —" Angela turned. "What's your name?"

"Dean." Dean didn't appear happy, and he said his name as if growing exhausted by her insulting inability to remember it.

Angela held her palms out as if subduing a raucous crowd and calling for calm, as if Willie was known for losing it and she had to take control and do double duty as the mature one. "Count to three, okay?"

Would he like her if she weren't his daughter? Would he even give her the time of day? At the moment he didn't know the answer. How frustrating to realize your kid had been sizing you up all their life and reaching the wrong conclusions. But then she had a knack for giving the subtlest spin to achieve maximum aggravation. "I'll do my best," he assured her in the most amused manner he could achieve.

"We had a bit of an accident," said Dean.

Sweat was spreading under the arms of Dean's white silk shirt. Willie regarded him and then returned his gaze to

Angela, making an effort to lid his eyes and relax his brow and breathe evenly. He awaited her version.

"We were on this hill," she said. "And there was all this sand —"

"She rear-ended me."

Willie subdued a spasm of anguish and reminded himself to relax. In a tone so calm, so mellow, so mild that he might have been remarking on the fine weather they were enjoying, he said, "Let's have a look." And so he left the chaos in the kitchen and accompanied Dean and Angela around to the front of the house to view the chaos there. Dean's emerald Volvo had indeed taken a whack, the rear bumper caved and the left taillight popped.

"Where's yours?"

"Going to need a wrecker," said Dean.

"My insurance'll go through the roof," said Angela.

Ah . . . Willie clued in. Gentleman Dean was willing to make a deal to preserve Angela's Safe Driving Discount. What a prince. He cocked an eyebrow at Dean, who, sensing a lack of gratitude on Willie's part, a failure to appreciate the gravity of the situation and who had the power here, began re-examining the damage. The results were troubling. "I don't know," he concluded. "Maybe we really ought to play this by the book." He looked to Willie as if appealing to him for his superior wisdom in these matters. "I mean, with whiplash you're fine at first, then —"

"How about a thousand?"

Dean performed well. He stayed in character and the pain was all his. "I'm really only thinking of Angela."

"Twelve."

Dean made noises.

"Fifteen."

Now Gentleman Dean became profound. He nodded slowly and considered the facts and concluded that yes, perhaps under the circumstances Willie's solution to the dilemma was for the best. "Alright. Fifteen hundred." He consulted his watch, a suede-strapped Rolex with more dials than an astrolabe. "I really have to run. So if we could take care of business . . ."

Urges warred in Willie's heart. Violence was an option, but this sort of guy would only bring in the law and he could ill afford such scrutiny. How about guilt? Could he at least infect Gentleman Dean's victory with enough guilt to make it throb with the festering fact of his sleaze? Willie jerked his thumb over his shoulder. "Just gimme a minute while I go inside and break the piggy bank."

Dean was nothing if not reasonable.

Carmen was waiting when Willie stumped up the back steps and into the kitchen. She followed him along the hall. "You bought her a car!" He got the last of his cash from the hollow in the side of the bedroom's folding closet door, fought Carmen off when she tried grabbing the money, locked himself in the bathroom and wrote out a cheque for twelve hundred dollars, then emerged and went back along the hall with Carmen beating his back like someone pounding a door, entered the kitchen and, in front of Angela, Rollo and Juliet, caught Carmen's fists and hugged her tight to calm her down and render her immobile. She squirmed but he held her in a bear hug and whispered, "Please don't torture me. Please. Help me. I beg you."

Her eyes filled with tears and her lip trembled. She heard the tone of his voice. He was pleading. "Oh, Willie," she said, and then she bit him on the neck deep enough to make him fear for his jugular.

～

When Dean had driven off with the cash and the cheque and a smile of contempt curling the corners of his thin-lipped mouth, Angela began to cry. Feeling empowered by the opportunity to provide fatherly solace as well as financial security, Willie put his arm around her shoulders and walked her around to the back-yard, sniffing as he went for any telltale odours from the crop. Nothing, just good old east-end air, parched and smoggy. At the foot of the steps Angela halted and squirmed out of his embrace as if his touch was a form of psoriasis.

Willie said, "Hey, it happens."

She thrust her jaw. "You've had accidents."

In fact Willie had never had a car accident. "I'll call a tow truck and we'll get the car right now."

They turned away from the house and crossed the lawn and got in the van. As he backed out he spotted Carmen on the porch. He rolled down the window and called, "Back in a minute!" Carmen made no acknowledgement, merely crossed her arms tightly and continued to glare.

～

As Willie drove, Angela stared off out the window in sullen silence. She had evolved into a tense and defiant young woman, independent, miserable, and as critical as she was insecure. Yet she'd made her trip to Asia alone, something Willie would never have ventured to do at her age or even now. Eight months through the Philippines, Thailand, Burma, India, Nepal. She returned even more defiantly independent, though at the same time with an element of maturity that registered itself in a new, if still fragile, sense of self-possession. He could only imagine what sort of adventures she'd had. Carmen guessed drugs, men, more drugs, more men, political demonstrations, seductive terrorists, and near fatal bus accidents in the Himalayas, whereas Willie, hopeful, naive, preferred to imagine quaint villages, the Taj Mahal, sunrise over the Ganges, solitary evenings in her hotel room reading *War and Peace*. Neither knew for sure because Angela was fiercely private about her personal life, and she made it clear that her travels were her own.

"That thing's disgusting," she said.

Willie didn't understand.

"On your neck. Your hickey."

He strained to see his neck in the mirror and saw the mark left by Carmen's bite. Willie watched the road and remained silent. He knew that he had a glutton's capacity to be used by others, who, like his daughter, like Juliet, like Rollo, had a gluttonous capacity to use, but he also endured the guilty realization that with this sort of relationship came power: it made him essential to their lives, he was the man with the cash, and cash made him important, for he could make things happen; they knew it and he knew it but no one dared mention it.

Angela said, "You're a criminal, you know."

Willie waited for her to laugh. She didn't. Was she ashamed of him? Was she scandalized? *Her*, his globe-trotting, pot-smoking, monk-fucking, anarchist daughter? "Is that what Gabriel said?"

She took offence. "I come to my own conclusions, thank you very much."

"That's good." His response had been prompt and his tone suggested that as her father he heartily approved, and now they could change topics. But now that the subject was open he wondered if Angela had told Gabriel what he was up to. Surely a hip old Psych prof who had lived in the Haight and partied with the Pranksters and travelled in India and Morocco was all for the Golden Herb. So he inquired, with an airy indifference, "What *does* Gabriel think, by the way?"

"Believe it or not, Dad, we don't talk about you."

Willie let the stab of pain flare then subside without reaction or remark. "We're not talking about heroin. Anyway, *you* smoke it."

Angela was unfazed. "Doesn't make it right. Besides, I need it. I'm scarred. I grew up in a broken home. My mother abandoned me and my grandmother hated me."

"Your grandmother was bitter at her husband. My father left, *that* was abandonment."

"Oh, right. Only you could be abandoned."

"She didn't hate you, she loved you." His mother had spent her last years in a robe and slippers, submerged in her misery like a flatfish in sand, enraged at anyone who hauled her up from the rich and silty depths of her self-pity. Still, Angela probably was scarred, and, as with most everything else, it was probably his fault. He wondered if she'd ever been in therapy and talked about him to some psychologist? Laid on some leather couch clutching a box of tissues and wept as she listed his misdeeds and the bruising she bore to this day?

Angela asked, "Did you *love* mom?"

Willie clenched the wheel and watched the road. His chin hardened and tears prickled in his eyes. Was she implying that he used the term love lightly, that he didn't know what it was? Love was too weak a word for what he'd felt for Mercedes. He'd worshipped her, he'd have swallowed battery acid for her, he'd have cut off his fingers, let rabid dogs rip into him if it would have won her love. His entire being had depended upon her approval and even now, a decade later, her memory could double him over with cramps. Add to that the humiliation of his grovelling phone calls, his letters, his drinking, his following her, his obsessing over her, his conviction that his life was finished, plus Angela's everlasting blame for his breaking up the family, add all this together and Willie's self-loathing was pretty much complete. "I love her," he said now, as if reciting the first line of a poem. "I *loved* her."

"Have you figured out why she dumped you?" She delivered the question as if she were the therapist and he the patient.

He said nothing, waiting for her to advance her own no-doubt-superior theory, but she remained silent. He and Angela had been close when she was small. He was always more attentive to her than Mercedes was, more patient, more concerned, and Angela used to climb into his lap and sit snuggled up against him — the clean smell of her hair and the heat of her body were still vivid in his mind — and watch cartoons, rooting for the coyote and hoping he'd finally catch the smug and aggravating roadrunner. On the rare occasions now when she drew in her claws and relented, it was as if the former Angela was re-emerging from within the demonic possession of embittered adulthood.

There was a hint of that now when she suddenly asked, with genuine curiosity, her voice rising at the end of the question, "Do you think she loved you?"

Willie battled a dizziness that blindsided him as if he'd been planked with a two-by-four. He tried not to veer into the oncoming traffic. A pragmatic loyalty was the closest Mercedes could come to loving another human being. He felt bad for her (how she would howl with scornful laughter at *that*) but he also felt a certain angry satisfaction that she was the flawed one — not him, her — and hoped that someday she would face it and endure an agony of regret over the way she'd treated him. Hoped, but doubted it would ever come to pass. When he thought of Mercedes he often thought of his father, not just because both had left, but because of how proud Willie would have been showing off such a stunning woman to his dad. As for his mother, she and Mercedes had always been awkward. She was glad he'd found someone, but suspicious as to how he'd done it, especially someone so absurdly gorgeous, and suspected that some of his father's slyness had slipped in through the filter of her genes. There was no secret to how he'd wooed and won Mercedes; he'd mortgaged his business and bought her a Victorian mansion in Shaughnessy, and he could pretty much pinpoint the first stage of Top Floor Construction's downfall to that ill-advised manoeuvre.

"Do you love this Gabriel?"

"Why is he always *this* Gabriel?"

Willie didn't know, maybe because he'd never met the guy, maybe because Angela alternately hid him then paraded him. "When am I going to meet him?" he asked, even though he didn't want to meet him, because he was terrified that Professor Gabriel would prove smarter, wittier, more stylish, more worldly, and of course fitter and better looking.

For her response, Angela opted to look away. "There it is there," she remarked, flat-voiced and grim.

When Willie saw the smashed Rabbit he nearly sobbed at the miracle of her walking away unharmed.

"Don't worry," she said, exhausted, bored. "I don't expect another one."

CHAPTER 5

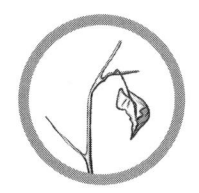

WHEN THEY GOT BACK, Ed Beebie next door was lighting his Hibachi. "Be in in a minute," Willie said to Angela, who wasn't waiting for him anyway. He watched her head inside and, defeated, exhausted, he crossed the lawn to have a word with his neighbour. "Ed."

"Young William." Ed was the only person other than his mother who'd ever called him William. Ed wore working greens with the sleeves rolled exposing forearms that, even at the age of seventy-three, were formidable. He met Willie at the fence that only last month they'd resurrected together, spending an afternoon replacing the pickets and reinforcing the posts, Ed painting his side and Willie doing his, all the while sipping beers and commenting on the quality of the wood and the paint and the brushes, with Ed occasionally quoting from his favourite book, *Meditations* by Marcus Aurelius. "'People exist for the sake of one another. Teach them then or bear with them.'" Yet at the moment he did not favour Willie with a pithy bit of wisdom. All he said was, "Saturday."

"Yeah?"

"Outta here." Ed gestured in a curiously graceful manner, like a little girl in the school play tracing the splendid arc of the rainbow, meaning far, far away, over the horizon and toward the fabled pot of gold at its end. He held a coffee in one hand and a Players Plain in the other. "Down the coast. *El camino.*" Ed stood close enough for the fumes of his breath to sear Willie's nostrils. Ed lived on cigarettes, caffeine and vodka, but what Ed thrived on was defiance. *Sixty-three years of smoking and here I am, you bastards, fifteen cups of coffee and two packs a day, and here I am! No tumours on me, no black spots on my lungs, good liver, clean kidneys, heart pumping steady as a slant six.* He'd done his time. No one could deny the fact that he'd put in forty-two long ones pounding a route for Canada Post. The mail sack had warped his spine and the memory of houses and mailboxes were stamped into his brain. Dig Ed up in a thousand years and recharge his frontal lobe and every dog and cat and kid, every housewife eating ice cream while watching Jack Lalane, would flicker to life.

"Scottsdale?"

"Naw." Ed winced at anything as bland as Scottsdale. His eyes narrowed against the light illuminating his private vision. His voice was edged with the sauciness of one savouring a secret. "Copper Canyon. Mexico."

"*Mexico?*"

Willie's admiration pleased Ed.

"I didn't know you were interested in Mexico."

Ed pitched the dregs from his mug and set it on the fence. The cup's caffeine-browned interior suggested a gas station toilet bowl overdue for a scrub. "Well, I wasn't. But I like to keep an open mind. 'All things are changing,'" he said, quoting Marcus Aurelius. He winked as if the profundity was simple to see. "And anyway I was watching one of these travel shows and I got kind of interested. It's deeper than the Grand Canyon."

Willie had never been to the Grand Canyon so had to make do with television images of gulches and vultures. But he nodded appreciatively.

"And there's these people," said Ed, leaning closer, his voice rising, his eyes rapt with wonder, "the Tarahumara Indians, they live in the canyons. And the thing is, these Indians, what they do is they run."

"Run?"

"Run for miles — a hundred miles — kicking a wooden ball."

Ed had been quite a soccer player in his youth, so would be impressed by Mexican Indians running miles through canyons kicking a wooden ball. And Willie, imagining it, could see the allure of these far off canyon people evolving their quirky culture, blithely indifferent to the world beyond, playing their game like splendid children graced with life eternal in their tropical garden. "Wow."

"Should come with me," said Ed. "Be fun." He nodded, hinting at all the trouble they could cause.

Accompanying Ed on down the coast to Mexico in the Winnebago didn't sound so bad, it would be a relief, he'd just sit back and enjoy the scenery. "My back's rough right now." Among the logistics Willie faced in becoming a pot farmer was what to tell the neighbours. What did he say when they leaned on their lawnmowers and asked what he did for a living? Computers were the first thing that came to mind, a job you could do from home, but Willie didn't fit the profile of programmer or writer. His hands were too thick and there was too much weather in his face. Phone sales? Accounting? Convalescing from an industrial accident? Yes. That was it. He'd honed that to permanent disability, a bad back, which was close to the truth, which was the key to successful lying. "Hurts to sit too long. Maybe if I walked to Mexico," he added in a rare flash of wit.

Ed never laughed at other people's jokes. When others made jokes he went silent as if they'd committed some indiscretion. He raised his head high stretching his wattles taut and kept his gaze upon the horizon and Mexico. "Well, you think about it."

"I will. I'd like to go," he added, wanting Ed to believe him, wanting Ed to like him. "Carmen's always on about it." And for the moment he indulged the idea of setting up in some seaside Mexican village with colonial architecture, learning the language and maybe getting a boat and taking people out fishing or bird watching. Willie got down to the reason for his visit. "Could I get a few briquettes from you?"

Ed was generosity personified. They proceeded along either side of the fence to the Winnebago door where he reached in and hauled out a jumbo sack of barbecue briquettes. "Take the bugger. I got three."

Willie felt obliged to take a minute and admire the artistry that had gone into the mural of the sand trap and putting green Ed had painted on the side of the Winnebago. He'd gone at the project with admirable patience and surprising craftsmanship. He fondly referred to the Winnebago as the Beast. Soon he'd be aiming the Beast south and stepping on the gas. The Beast had a stainless steel sink, cove-top counters, microwave, thirty-six-inch TV, and the mock-mahogany panelling that Willie had always gone to great lengths to talk people out of.

"Everything you need in there," observed Willie.

"Except a little companionship," he said, indicating the double bed. He winked and — was that a touch of the palsy — or did Ed give a thrust of his hips?

Willie felt betrayed, as if he'd caught a favourite uncle masturbating. He wanted Ed to be old and wise and concerned with things higher than the crotch. Yet why shouldn't old Ed have a girlfriend? Healthy guys Ed's age had their pick of the blue-hairs because men died earlier than women, or were all stroked out and drooling. So where were all the elderly ladies clamouring to go to dinner with Ed, bake him pies, make the bingo scene, embark on cruises? In the cruel light of afternoon, Ed wasn't exactly Marcello Mastroianni, but then again he was not exactly an ogre. Coffee-breath aside, he was always cleanly shaved and bore about him the aroma of soap. His wiry hair was full and thick. He had a ruggedly corrugated forehead and a good straight nose free of the booze blossoms that plagued so many drinkers. He kept his swearing to a minimum and, as a devotee of Marcus Aurelius, he was stoic about the aches that accompanied old age. Ed's wife had "died on him" eleven years ago. He'd never explained why they'd had no kids and Willie didn't press. He knew that the essence of friendship was knowing what *not* to ask, where *not* to pry, which topics to leave untouched: an agreement of *I won't challenge you if you won't challenge me.*

Mexico. Well. Ed had spark yet. Willie imagined the idea of Mexico flaring Bic-like in Ed's brain and making him sit upright on his sagging couch. It was perfect, it made sense, the door was opening and he was steppin' on through.

"First stop I'll visit Diane just over the border. Connie's sister's daughter. Haven't seen her since the funeral. Spend a few days then head south. Take her as she comes."

"She's the one with the farm?"

"Widow at forty-eight." Ed fixed Willie with a formidable gaze and Willie became dutifully solemn, for an important fact was forthcoming. "Husband was only fifty-one years old."

"Fifty-one?"

Ed nodded profoundly, and then they shook their heads at the tragedy of it. Fifty-one years old. The very thought terrified Willie. "Hurt her. Hurt her bad," said Ed, eyes shiny with tears. Willie grew awkward and wondered if he should pat the old guy's shoulder. Then Ed sighed and brightened. "Got a nice place, rundown, but a lot of character. Fruit trees, beehives, garden. You ever get down across the line you should pop in. Just opposite a trailer park."

Willie nodded.

"Maybe she'll come to Mexico with me."

Willie smiled; he hoped so. He'd have liked to spend the rest of the long summer evening enjoying a few vodkas and hearing stories about Ed's childhood in Vancouver during the Great Depression, yet Angela started screaming in the kitchen, her voice as shrill as a saw blade shrieking through sheet metal, so Willie bid Ed goodbye.

CHAPTER 6

ANGELA HAD HATED CARMEN since before they even met. "An *artist*? You call this narcissistic crud *art*?" Angela's first look at the sixty-three self-portraits dominating her father's walls had inspired an incredulous sneer. She'd strolled from the kitchen to the living room, down the hall into and out of the bathroom, and then back to the living room again, shaking her head the entire time. "This is psychosis. She's sick, Dad, can't you see it?" Rarely had Willie seen such a mix of disgust and disbelief on the same human face, and rarely had he seen Angela lost for words. Reduced to gesturing, she'd raised her hands and let them drop with a slap against her thighs. "You're surrounded!" Willie had admitted that while Carmen's subject range was narrow, her talent and draughtsmanship were undeniable. Angela's response was that this only made it more shameless.

Now they were at it again. Willie plodded loudly up the wooden stairs and took up a position in the kitchen doorway with his hands on his hips hoping his impressive presence would shut Carmen and Angela up. They ignored him.

Angela flung her arm indicating the paintings. "This isn't art, it's dementia. You're demented!" Angela put her finger to her temple and made a screwing motion.

Carmen took strength in the fact that the self-portrait was a valid and time-honoured genre. Everyone from Dürer to Rembrandt to Goya to Van Gogh had painted them, why not her? "So, the radical young miss has opinions on art, does she?"

Willie stepped between them and thrust out his arms like a ref separating fighters. "Enough." He risked a long exhalation of incredulity and disgust, and in a voice of quiet reason reminded them, "We have a crop of pot in the basement and it might be wise not to attract too much attention."

"You bought her a car."

"Carmen —"

"That was generous," said Carmen in an even voice. "You are a generous man." She looked at him with the fullest sincerity, and then she looked at the others: Rollo at the kitchen table enjoying the sexual thrill from the spectacle of overexcited females, Juliet sitting across from him with her book of crossword puzzles, and finally Angela, sneering in the archway that led to the living room. "Isn't he a generous man? Yes, he is. He is indeed generous. But I ask you, Willie: who spent the last three days trimming for you? Who got a rash? Who's getting carpal tunnel syndrome? Angela? Not likely. No, I am. Me."

"Me, me, me," mocked Angela. "*Mee-mee-mee*! The only song you know, isn't it? Like your idiotic pictures. You need a psychiatrist, cow!"

Carmen ignored this and proceeded in that smooth voice of utter reasonableness. "My hands are numb, Willie. I can't feel my fingers. That's nerve damage. How am I supposed to paint? I ask you, how do I paint with numb fingers? I'm an artist. I need my hands. Some people may question my content, fine, but I display my pictures in galleries. I work hard and I get reviewed. I am not some hack who sits in Stanley Park on Sunday afternoon doing blue barnyards with a palette knife. And those surgical gloves we use? They're plastic. Plastic causes cancer. My skin's been absorbing the molecules."

Angela shut her eyes in disbelief. "*Surgical gloves cause cancer?*" Did the absurdity never end? How could she be in the same room as this woman? "Carmen, you are so fucking ignorant. Do us all a favour and go back to Surrey."

This only made Carmen even more serene. She wasn't going to get snagged on the rocks of that old taunt. Surrey had been bucolic when she'd grown up there. *Her* Surrey bore no resemblance to the sprawl of beige condos and fluorescent shopping malls breeding alienated teenagers responsible for the highest rate of car thefts in North America. Carmen's stepfather had been the Right Reverend Henry Robert Bancroft of the Four Square United Pentecostal Church of North Surrey after whom, yes *whom*, a street was named, not to mention a minimall and a high school scholarship, the Henry R. Bancroft Excellence Award. That was pedigree, that was lineage. So she merely smiled and shook her head in deepest sympathy for how poor Willie must suffer over the spectacle that Missy Angela was once again making of herself. "Young lady, you are one queen-sized bag of bad karma."

"Karma? *Karma?*" Angela gagged. "I'm the one who went to India. Me, Carmen — *me*! You don't even know what karma is."

"Enough," said Willie.

But Carmen intended to complete her defence. "I worked hard, Willie. I worked hard for the past three days. Maybe my work was not up to your exacting standards, but I laboured. I was there. And for months now I have lived with risk. How often has she shown her face in that time? Don't strain yourself, Willie: once. Today. When she needs something."

"You sat on your fat ass and whined," said Angela. "Dad told me."

Angela had scored a knockout blow that flattened Carmen and punctured the very room itself. The air fled, leaving a crackling vacuum. Willie did not have time to point out Angela's blatant lie because he was too busy ducking the flung cup of Chablis that hit the centrepiece of Carmen's triptych dislodging it from the wall. The picture dropped to the table and the glass facing fractured like stomped ice.

"Carmen! Wait! I never said —"

But she was already out the door and down the steps. Willie followed her onto the porch and watched her cross the lawn. "Carmen!"

Angela joined him on the porch. "Hey, Carm, I think that's called an Avoidance Manoeuvre!"

Willie whirled on his daughter with his hand raised as if to clap her across the skull. He halted and the two of them remained frozen. Angela's fright at having so blatantly overstepped herself widened her eyes so that Willie saw not a twenty-four-year-old woman but his four-year-old daughter. Without a word, he turned and went down the stairs two at a time and caught Carmen in the alley.

Carmen did not struggle or shout or fuss when he gripped her arm, she merely gazed at him with eyes so forlorn that Willie crumbled. Her voice was faint, as if she were already far away, banished to the land of the unloved.

"Carmen."

"I need to think, Willie. I need to think." And in the manner of one taking leave forever, of one pulled by the inexorable wind of loss, she walked slowly away, shoulders round and weak and unsuited to the burdens of the world.

❦

Willie swung open the fridge door and searched for a beer. He shifted the hot sauce and mayonnaise and Czech mustard and soy sauce and the jars of roll-mops and dills, the Tupperware containers of unrecognizable leftovers, the Chinese food still in its paper-lidded foil containers, but all the beer, all his Pilzn Urquells, the best beer in the world, the only beer in the world, the beer that made life liveable, were gone. He turned. Rollo, five empties arranged in a star in front of him, paused with the last bottle part way to his mouth.

"Buddy, hey." In an act of large-hearted magnanimity, Rollo wiped the bottle's mouth and held it out to Willie. "You need it."

Using two fingers, he removed the bottle from Rollo's grip as if drawing it from an acid bath, took a long drink then dropped to one of the kitchen chairs, an old tube-metal effort with yellow vinyl and stars that matched the table. Carmen and Willie had bought it together, indulging the retro wave that, like a returning tide, had brought back the flotsam of a bygone era. He regarded Angela who had retreated to the far wall and could not meet his gaze.

Juliet sighed now because the time had come for her to step forward and sort everything out. Along with the grim reality of her long gone youth and faded beauty, age, like an unwelcome guest, brought burdens of responsibility: she was obliged to be wise. She clucked her tongue, lay her pencil alongside her crossword puzzle — the theme, '70s sitcoms — and directed her gaze at Willie. "Well?"

"Well, what?"

"Don't be a dip, Willie. You can't let her wander around. She'll get drunk and she'll talk." Juliet kept her eyes on Willie to be sure he understood the car-out-of-control consequences of Carmen adrift. Stern-eyed and severe, not even the lifelong overindulgence in booze, coke, pot, sun, sex and all-night parties could mask the fact that Juliet had been a stunner. She'd partied in London and San Francisco and Mexico City, sailed the Caribbean, been treated to Club Med more times than she could count, blown spliff in Kingston with Bob Marley, and done Mardi Gras in Vera Cruz. The indignity of declining beauty had made her regal, a Roman empress of terrible prowess. Not that this was any solace to Juliet. At her age, she was beyond the reach of Amazonian oils and muds from the

Mekong Delta to restore the complexion of her youth. She did have one last hope, however, one final stay of execution: a Santa Barbara spa called Athena featuring hormone treatments, and a process called oxyjuvenation that involved polyphenols and the anti-aging enzyme sirtuin. The problem was that even the briefest stay — one weekend, Friday evening to Sunday afternoon — cost four thousand nine hundred and ninety-nine U.S. dollars. For a woman living on welfare topped up with the five hundred a month Willie gave her, this spa was but the cruellest mirage dancing beyond her reach. Perhaps even crueller was the fact that Mercedes, her own daughter, Willie's ex and Angela's mother, declined to give her so much as a dime despite having access to the bottomless wealth of an Argentinean millionaire named Oscar. The notion that Juliet might seek — much less find — a job was only slightly less absurd than Mercedes returning from Buenos Aires and showing up in East Vancouver begging Willie to take her back.

"She's just taking a walk."

"*Willie.*" Juliet trapped his hand and pressed it to the table, grounding him in the reality he so clearly wished to avoid. She leaned forward causing the beads in her dreads to swing and click, bringing with her a scent of frangipani. "She's unstable."

She was right. He knew what Carmen was capable of. Carmen had delighted in describing what she did when Art — husband number two — cheated on her. First she moved out, taking his TV and CD player and digital camera, then she returned with a dozen pork chops and hid them throughout the condo, behind the baseboards, in the attic, wedged behind the facings of the light switches. Art was not only Jewish but a vegan, who refused to even allow meat products on his property much less in his kitchen. When the pork began to rot the stench hit and the vermin arrived. Every time Carmen told the story she laughed until she cried. *He was hysterical. He was shrieking. He was in tears. He was running around in gumboots and overalls and a gas mask spraying the walls with insecticide. He had to sell the place. But before that he had to tear out walls!*

"She's schizo," Angela added.

"Give it a rest," said Willie.

"She's a freak."

He raised his voice to threat level. "*Angela.*" Though what he would threaten he had no idea. He thought of the Rabbit: three weeks and totalled. He thought of Rollo and his usurious rent, of Juliet and the five hundred dollars a month he gave her, of the BMW he'd promised Carmen and the studio he'd promised her. And now add the fifteen hundred he'd just given Gentleman Dean the Extortionist. He drank his Pilzn Urquell to the dregs and tried to feel drunk. With the strongest voice he could muster he said, "She'll be back in an hour or so."

Juliet's eyes — as azure as the Caribbean, as cutting as coral — gauged him. She arched one of her perfectly plucked brows. Willie struggled to maintain her gaze but his eyes began to prickle. Juliet was at her ease, for this was her territory, the cruel and concrete reality of social chess, a game at which, despite her current obscurity, she'd once been grandmaster. "And if she isn't back in an hour?"

"She's got no money and she's on foot."

Juliet refused to be diverted. "And if she isn't?"

Before Willie could consider the extent to which Carmen could undermine the entire operation by the right word to the wrong person, Rollo suddenly discovered his watch. "Jesus, look at that," he cried as if it was not a wristwatch on his arm but a scorpion. Backing out the door, he jerked his thumb over his shoulder indicating a world of obligations that would topple without his immediate attention.

Willie followed him onto the porch and down the steps. "Look, about this rent business."

"Hey, you want to cut me out of the loop . . ." Rollo shrugged the shrug of the innocent victim. Now Willie felt bad. Rollo put his hands deep into his pockets and gazed around nostalgically. "Man, I used to cut this lawn with a push mower, one of those old ones with the steel wheels. For a quarter, I did it for a quarter." He shrugged again and then he remembered something else. "Oh, yeah. I was gonna tell you. You need a fast few hundred I know a barn show's coming down tomorrow. Out in the valley. Probably two days' work. Thirty-an-hour. Come outta there with five-maybe-six bills." He spoke simply, offering a small gift.

Five hundred dollars would not solve Willie's problems, but it would buy him time until the crop was sold. "You gonna be there?"

"Tomorrow's Friday, man. I don't know about you, but I have to work."

"Right, right." Rollo was oddly responsible when it came to laying carpet. Maybe he was addicted to the fumes and loved kneeling on those plush new rolls, taking deep breaths. Willie didn't like the idea of trimming for people he didn't know. "They're okay?"

Rollo turned his hands palm upward: would he recommend them if they weren't? "Anyway. Up to you." He turned and started across the lawn to his van parked in the alley.

Willie watched him go and then followed, a hopeful anxiety simmering in his stomach. He had to give the crop three days to dry, then a night to let Lars hike it across the border, then wait for Dwayne to rendezvous with Rollo and pay up. That would be a week, minimum, seven days of Carmen riding him. Dropping a quick five hundred into her lap would pave a lot of rough road. He rubbed his stubbled jaw and glanced around. The sun was behind the rooftops and the shadows had crept from their hiding places and were crawling across the lawn. Five hundred dollars. "Two days trimming?"

Rollo halted at the gate and shrugged like what was easier, but then who knew, he was but a humble man taking his knocks in a hard world.

"Okay. I'll give you a cut. You know, a finder's fee."

Rollo gestured that away. "I'll call you later with the address. Oh, by the way, just so you know, most guys charge two hundred bucks commission per pound, not one."

CHAPTER 7

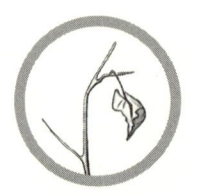

JULIET WAS WAITING IN THE kitchen with a raw steak skewered on a barbecue fork. She raised her arm and, with the slab of meat, indicated the minefield of the urban night. "You cannot leave that woman wandering loose."

That woman . . . This was more than a little insulting. Juliet had never had a cross word with Carmen, not because they got along, but because Juliet did not lower herself to such unseemly grappling. "She'll be back."

Juliet offered a dry stare.

"She will," he said, bolstering his voice with a conviction he did not have. He escaped into the living room where he clicked on the TV and checked his watch. Five past seven. Oh, God! He was missing *Home Sweet Home*.

He hated *Home Sweet Home*. Putting his feet up on the coffee table, he crossed his ankles and got comfortable. "Look at the asshole," said Willie aloud, even though Angela and Juliet were off in the kitchen. There was Ross Lyndon with his permed hair, ear stud, tailored denim shirt, tool belt, that laddish smile of his, and of course the dimples — Willie suspected Ross shoved dimes edgewise into his dimples to deepen them — the Brad Pitt of home improvement.

"Today we're going to talk about linoleum. The key to successful lino is this." Ross flashed his measuring tape like a badge. "As my dad used to say, measure twice, cut once. Now let's see what kind of mess we can make." And with that, he gave his signature Ross Lyndon wink, which made Willie bark with scorn.

"Look at him. Just look at him! When he worked for me he didn't even know which end of the hammer to use." Willie crossed his arms tightly over his chest and concentrated as the camera followed Ross into a bathroom.

Ross held up the tape measure once again, as if it were a compass that would guide him through times of storm and stress. "You tile —"

"From the centre out," said Willie. "Find the middle point of the room and work out to the walls. Duh." He shouted, "Hey Ross, where'd you learn that, huh? Why don't you tell them who taught you everything you know? And while you're at it, tell them about the Gyproc you wasted, the windows you dropped, the glue you spilled, the paint you kicked over, how you whined during the winter and complained during the summer, and oh yeah, show them your hand where you nearly cut your fingers off because you don't know a Skilsaw from a see-saw." Willie blew air and shook his head. Ross Lyndon owed his success to his face. The only solace came from the knowledge that the guy's dream was to be an actor, a real actor, not Mr. Handyman. But that was worse in a way because it demeaned the craft. Willie could have brought authenticity and love to the show. *Willie's Workshop. Working with Willie.* But with *his* mug?

When *Home Sweet Home* ended, the news came on. Lola Winter, celebrity-anchorwoman, recently featured on the cover of *West Coast Woman*, wife of TV chef and restaurateur Cosmo Calvino, looking sleek and chic in her signature blue and gold, swivelled to face the camera and donned her serious-story voice for the next segment, which concerned a marijuana bust.

"Vancouver police are patting themselves on the back today," began Lola as the camera cut to footage of a basement, not unlike Willie's own, full of pot plants — though the plants were not nearly as bushy or vibrant or happy as his babies. In the one quick camera pass Willie observed that the people behind the crop were amateurs. To start with they were growing in dirt instead of clay balls, their lights were unhooded, the place was chaos, and there was no reservoir or cooling system, which meant the plants were susceptible to all manner of waterborne fungus. A shoddy set-up. Lola Winter — half million-a-year-anchorwoman, her taupe Mazeratti awaiting in the premier spot in the station's parking salon where it received its daily wash, wax and detailing — was now informing her viewers that the police were designating it a "high-tech system that could yield half a million dollars per crop."

The outrageousness of this jerked Willie out of his seat as if he'd been yanked by a wire. "Lies!"

A police officer with a well-scrubbed moustache and a grave manner pointed to the clone room, a closet with a few trays of sprout-sized seedlings, solemnly declaring how each of those seemingly innocent plantlets would produce a thousand dollars of the deadly marijuana that lured girls and boys to the crack house of doom.

Willie's hands flailed in spastic frustration at the blatant misinformation.

"They're stroking their dicks for the public," said Juliet coming in with a platter of steaks.

"You don't measure a crop's yield by plant," Willie shouted at the burr-headed cop. "You measure it by lamp! And half those clones'll die anyway. And as for those pathetic plants —" he was disgusted "— there was no bud. It was all salad. They'll be lucky to see five pounds of leaves. *Half a million bucks.* What bunk. What crud. What shite. And there was way too much phosphorus. Did you see that? The leaves were burnt. They think they can just pile on the fertilizer and boom — bud. They were all stalk. They waited too long before cutting back to twelve hours."

But Lola Winter hadn't finished. She had repaired to the Moave Room where she was joined by alderman Harry Shoe, former RCMP constable turned Roman Catholic priest Father Ivan Gurniak, and SFU sociologist Francine Cunningham. Willie turned up the volume.

"Welcome to you all," said Lola. "Ivan Gurniak, let's start with you. You have a unique perspective, having been on both sides of the fence so to speak. First as a law enforcement officer, and now as a priest who runs a parish in the infamous Downtown Eastside, a neighbourhood notorious for having the highest rates of drug-related violence, addiction and disease in all Canada. Father Gurniak, should marijuana be decriminalized much less legalized?"

Willie mouthed a silent *No*. Legalization would put him out of business.

The priest's nose was bent, his eyebrows were frayed wires and his face creased with the wear of a man who knew the grit of the street. He spread his arms as if calling on the faithful for their patience and understanding. "I would rephrase the question: is addiction a crime? No. Not at all. Addiction is a symptom of despair and despair is the deepest of sins for it denies God." He gazed forlornly at Diane who feigned to dwell deeply upon this.

"Why would a man become a priest?" wondered Juliet.

"I think it's kind of sexy," said Angela, sitting down with her plate in her lap.

Willie, aghast that his little girl could find anything sexy, coughed his food onto his plate.

"Alderman Harry Shoe? Decriminalize marijuana?"

Shoe bore an uncanny resemblance to a young and athletic Dan Rather, his eyes fierce to the verge of feverish, his voice resonant with conviction. "Absolutely not, Lola. Absolutely not. I talk to my constituents every day and the message I get over and over is *no*. Parents, single mothers, concerned citizens, hardworking people of all race, creed, colour, and persuasion are scared. And it's not just fear of the dope dealer on the corner, but little Jimmy's ex-hippie father who leaves drugs lying around in the rumpus room, who uses drugs in front of his family, who thinks he knows more than the experts. And the experts are very clear."

"Francine Cunningham?"

Judging by her short drab hair and bleak grey clothes, Francine Cunningham was well on her way to achieving her goal of asexuality. "Well, the Amsterdam experiment —"

"Is an unmitigated disaster," cut in Alderman Shoe. "The numbers are in — it failed, it flopped, it did not work. Addiction and related crime are higher than ever."

"I challenge your source, Alderman Shoe. Amsterdam's HIV rates are in fact half Vancouver's. Their rates of violent crime are down across the board. All the progressive social democracies are implementing similar programs. But I want to make another point. We must understand that the urge to seek ecstatic experience — whether by drugs, prayer, dance, whatever — is common to all cultures and should not be punished."

"In a religious context," cautioned the priest. "Otherwise it's mere escapism."

Alderman Shoe had shut his eyes and was shaking his head as if he'd heard it too many times before. "Lola, Lola, Lola. This sort of academic bafflegab is exactly what the good people of this city are sick and tired of hearing. It's why I stand for cuts to higher education and favour redirecting funds to the trade schools where our young men and women will be trained and certified with the practical skills needed to face not only the future but the ever-increasing competition from Asia." Assuming control of the interview, Shoe demanded, "Miss

Cunningham. Let me ask you a simple question: Do you or do you not condone drug use?"

"I do not condone drug *abuse*."

"Drug use *is* drug abuse."

The sad-eyed Professor Cunningham understood that she was engaged in a religious discussion rather than a policy debate. She looked exhausted, as if Shoe's very existence enfeebled her. "Do you use aspirin, Alderman Shoe? Do you drink an occasional glass of wine?"

"You cannot compare wine and aspirin to heroin."

"And you cannot compare heroin to marijuana," countered Cunningham.

"Let's move on, shall we?" said Lola. "Father Gurniak, if legalization is unlikely, and tougher penalties are not the answer, what do *you* propose?" She gave the priest a seriously searching expression, one she'd practised and would no doubt like to see on the cover of her upcoming biography.

"First let me assure you I believe in the rule of law. But we live in a stressful society —"

This was too much. "Father, all of us face stress," said Alderman Shoe. "I face stress, you face stress, the birds in the trees face stress. Yet I do not see sparrows injecting detergent-laced chemicals into their arteries and mugging old ladies."

The priest exhaled formidably. "Our police force is under-staffed and our jails are over-full," he stated in a voice he'd surely employed to good effect in his years as a cop. "Prisons are expensive and they fail to correct. And yet you favour piling more work onto the police and more people into the jails. News flash, Alderman: people are not junk metal. However much you and your sort would like to get rid of them, they cannot be melted down and turned into tin cans. Time is running out!"

"It is indeed," said Lola Winter. "Alderman Shoe, Father Gurniak, Professor Cunningham, I thank you all for coming. Stay with us for Brad Keen and sports. Brad, how about those Expos?"

After supper Juliet rolled a spliff while Angela plucked a Matinée from her grandmother's pack.

Willie said, "Since when do you smoke?"

Angela moued as if she'd been asked since when could she tie her own shoes. While Juliet completed construction on a colossal reefer, Angela sorted through the CDs and found *Toots and the Maytals*, her Christmas gift to Willie last year. The beat boomed up big and Angela began to bob while Juliet struck a match and toked once, twice, three times, until the end glowed and crackled like a pagan fire. She offered it to Willie who shook his head. "No thanks."

Angela held her hand out. "Me, me, me."

He hated Angela smoking, and he especially hated the leather-lunged performance tokes she was now executing for their benefit. *Yes, yes, Angela, we know what an old herb-head you are.* With her buzz up and running, she passed the reefer, eased back into the hot bath of her high, and began nodding to the slowest beat. How could Willie begrudge his little girl some relief? She needed a path into the balmy garden of bliss where she could wander free of her burdens.

Juliet toked, then offered it again to Willie who declined again.

"What's wrong?"

He worked to keep the pique out of his voice. "Nothing's *wrong*, Angela." At one time he'd smoke up and the world moved in close and sensual like a cat rubbing his leg. He could smoke alone and suddenly not feel lonely because the world itself became intimate, as if attracted to him, as if it liked being around him, but that was thirty-odd years ago, back when he was a teenager, in the days when a reefer was a door that magically appeared in the brick wall surrounding his life and he could step on through into the sunlight and bask. Pot was a dazzling backwater that he could visit while everyone else elbowed for ego room in the grit and blare of the fuck-you world. Nowadays if he smoked he felt lost. It was a relationship that had soured, those golden days gone like a lover who'd grown bored.

"Did you smoke a hookah on your travels?" asked Juliet. "I always wanted to smoke a hookah, with those long silk-wrapped tubes. Willie, have you ever —" But she dismissed him with a wave. "You've never done anything." Juliet and Angela shared a grin.

Why was it that when three people got together two always ganged up on one? He narrowed his eyes and retreated deep inside the cave of himself, biding his time. Willie had the tenacity of a slug crossing a hot road. He would get there or wither in the process. He would make his money and get his orchard, and, alone if need be, stroll beneath the fruit-sweet trees in summer, admire their golden leaves in the fall, watch their snow-fringed limbs in winter, breathe the scent of the blossoms in spring. He would do that, he vowed to himself. And he would travel some day, not to India or Burma or Jamaica but to Pilzn, in the Czech Republic, where he would tour the 700-year-old brewery, home of Pilzn Urquell.

"I've smoked a hookah lotsa times," said Angela. "I'll get you one. Who really needs it though is Miss What's-her-name." She thrust her chin at Carmen's self-portraits covering the wall.

For a moment they all considered them. Carmen with a rose. Carmen as seen through mist. Carmen in profile nose-to-nose with Carmen in profile. Carmen laughing. Carmen troubled. Carmen hugging her shins with her chin on her knees contemplating a daisy. Even Willie had to admit that this series — the one all-consuming life's work upon which she was embarked — suggested a disturbing degree of self-attention.

Angela now made a show of counting the pictures, her voice growing more amazed and incredulous as the number climbed. "Thirty-seven. Do you believe this? Thirty-seven self-portraits in this room alone!" She clapped her hands over her eyes as if they burned. "I can't bear it. Can we at least turn them so they face the wall? I mean, really. How do you stand it, Dad? It's like being stuck right inside her head!"

Willie grew irritated while Juliet merely ignored her. Willie envied Juliet, who had no fear of losing Angela's loyalty and therefore wouldn't.

"So." Juliet checked her watch and then cast Willie a questioning gaze. "Where is she?"

With the dishes dumped in the sink beneath a halo of soap, Willie accompanied Juliet and Angela around the side of the house and out along the cracked cement walkway to Juliet's Cadillac. She was a 1959 Fleetwood Sixty Special sedan, with whitewall tires, fins like a shark, and more chrome than Burt Lancaster had teeth. Despite lack of funds the car was as doggedly maintained as Juliet herself. It had white paint and red leather interior, and was moored yachtlike next to the sidewalk. The car was the gift of a former lover, Jean Luc Charbonier, a Haitian businessman who represented a sweatshop that manufactured baseballs for the National League, the last man of any status to worship at the altar of Juliet's beauty. Not only had he given her the car, but he had inspired in her a genuine interest in the game of baseball. Aside from memories, broken bits of jewellery and empty perfume bottles, the car was all that she had left from her life as a courtesan.

Every time Willie saw the car, he was impressed in the same way he was impressed anew by the sight of Juliet's looks. He stroked the Cadillac's flank and nodded his approval.

"Needs a tune-up," observed Juliet, knowing Willie loved the car. Only last month he'd forked out for a set of new tires, original whitewalls that had to come from back east, and he'd also replaced the key she'd lost and gotten her one of those magnet-holders so she could stash the new spare under the rear bumper.

Willie said he'd see how things stacked up after the sale. He'd come through and she knew it, but he reserved the right to at least reflect upon it and Juliet was shrewd enough to grant him this.

Angela swung open the door and tumbled onto the seat.

"When are you heading back down to Seattle?"

"Couple of days."

He waited for Angela to suggest they get together before then, but the seconds ticked past and she made no such suggestion. How exhausting. Now all that remained was the awkward hug that felt as if he was embracing a hat rack, and was all the more clumsy for her already being in the car. Juliet opened the door and, starlet that she was, arranged herself behind the wheel and switched on the ignition. "Find her, Willie."

"I will."

"You'd better."

Watching them pull away, Willie imagined their sighs of relief. He was supporting them both and yet they froze him out. They swiped bud from him thinking he was too dim to notice, and were probably firing some up at that very moment, not caring that the bud was green, just glad to get away, singing along to some reggae tune, cruisin' in the Caddie like a couple of teenagers. Still, he insisted on believing that Juliet respected him — sort of. He footed her bills and had been good to Mercedes, maybe not good *for* her, or not good *enough* for her, but good *to* her, and that counted for something. Or did Juliet dismiss him as a fool?

Angela thought he was a fool, but didn't all kids judge their parents fools? Did Angela ever suspect the sort of discussions her own mother and grandmother had about her? Or, humiliated, did she nightmare about it? *No boobs. No bum. Short teeth. Complexion like cardboard. And that hair — like seaweed. Oh, well, maybe she's better off without the attention. . . .* Juliet pitied her, and Mercedes was embarrassed by her. Glancing from Mercedes to Angela, and back to Mercedes, more than one person had assumed that Angela was adopted and asked if she was "one of those Romanian babies?" Bombshell mother and grandmother, and yet here she was, woof-woof city, and Willie was to blame. On Angela's fourteenth birthday, Mercedes had carted her off for a massive makeover, an entire day frowned at and brooded over by teams of be-smocked women who conferred and clucked and circled her then went at the job of oiling and baking and scraping and plucking and smoothing and mudding. By the end of the day — and four hundred and sixty-five dollars later — Angela had returned in tears, and Mercedes shelved her like some aggravating puzzle. Willie and Mercedes had argued while Angela wept, but whose approval did she crave, whose opinion mattered?

CHAPTER 8

THE PRINCETON HOTEL stood opposite the waterfront tracks, and as Willie walked toward it he heard the clash of coupling rail cars, the clap and roar of the grain elevators, and smelled the rancid-lard stench from the rendering plant. Not the neighbourhood he'd choose for a drink these days, but in the past two hours he'd looked everywhere.

He pulled open the pub door and entered the realm of false hope: pull tabs, lotto, and the possibility of romance. The pub had been upgraded from the days when Willie had used to drink here. The terrycloth and linoleum had been replaced by oak, cedar, and brass. But it was the same clientele: longshoremen, sailors, old men from the Powell Street rooming houses and anorexic hookers, locust-lean in spandex hot pants, their pelvic bones sharp enough to flay a deer. As he entered he saw a bald man seated with his back to the wall reading the *Daily Racing Form*. The guy glanced up and regarded Willie for an instant then resumed his study of the running lines. There was something familiar about him. Willie chanced another look. The man's gaze flickered up then bore down harder on the page. He had a thick moustache, a thick nose, and thick eyebrows.

At one table sat half a dozen Chinese sailors, each with a plastic bag of shopping spree loot; at another, a woman had passed out with her face on her arm while her companion gazed at a black-and-white photo on the wall — proud loggers lined like sparrows along a fallen cedar of titanic diameter. And there, in a corner by a window that looked out over the tracks and the container-stacked docks, sat Carmen, not Carmen alone and forlorn, but *Carmen and a man*. Willie's view of the man in question was partially blocked, but he could tell the guy was short, which offered some — but not a lot of — reassurance. Willie was no fighter. The very thought of confrontation earned him a squirt of stomach acid and a range of humiliating scenarios: the guy decking him, Carmen pitching her beer in his face, Carmen putting her arm around the guy and announcing they were flying to Mexico City.

She was laughing and gesturing with a cigarette in one hand and a beer in the other as if in the midst of telling a joke. When she saw Willie her expression went flat. Her companion turned: Rollo.

If Rollo nearly choked on a clot of panic, he swallowed it down too fast for Willie to notice. In moments of crisis, Rollo could gulp back his own bile and vomit, his heart, his pride and his very soul, so that his moods could shift from fear to delight as smoothly as if applied with a roller, leaving only the high gloss of his grin. He took charge of the situation. He smiled and kicked a chair toward Willie. "Siddown. Beer?" Before Willie could answer, Rollo was scanning for a waiter. "Stavros. Hey. Three more rockets right here, man." Then Rollo leaned closer to impart the good news. "All set."

"What is?"

Rollo reacted as if Willie were showing signs of Alzheimer's. "The trim. Tomorrow. Dude was just here. Lance. Didn't you see him? Tall. That's why I'm here, buddy. Ding, ding, ding. To help you out." He grinned and shook his head at Willie-the-amnesiac. As Willie was about to raise the issue of this most curious coincidence that found them all together, Rollo was flipping a coaster like a dealer laying a deuce, clicking his Paper Mate and scrawling the address. He hooked the pen over his collar and then mimed a riff on an upright bass. "Gigging here next week." His fingers danced a drum roll on the table edge. With a sweep of his palm he painted a banner. "*Rockin' Rollo and the All-Stars*. You coming?"

Willie looked at Carmen who was smoking with gusto, defying him to say a word about it. She exhaled a jet of smoke, arched one eyebrow, and regarded him. Willie waited, breath held, for her to lob some poison-tipped dart. Whatever she intended to do, she was diverted by the spectacle of a couple staggering onto the dance floor, the man as lean as a rope, with a pencil-thin moustache and rings on his fingers, the woman bursting her spandex, the fabric squirming under the strain, her face so vast and pale and Arctic that her red lips were a crushed rose in the snow. When the beers arrived, Rollo clinked Willie's glass and winked.

"Rollo thinks Mexico's a great idea," said Carmen.

Willie had no doubt.

❦

Willie fed their cat, Boyd, a fat black male who no longer bothered to hunt, spending most of his time on Willie and Carmen's bed, or behind the furnace in the basement where he satisfied his occasional need for greens by nibbling at the pot plants. It intrigued Willie to think that Boyd had been there when the poachers had come in and ripped off his crop. He recalled how in some old-time detective story, maybe Dick Tracy, Dick had seen the killer's face frozen in the pupils of the dead man. Willie had tried it, picking up Boyd — a drooping sack of cat — and, peering into his eyes, sought the lingering retinal image of who'd done the dirty on him. Willie found only a pair of blank and unblinking eyeballs. Thirteen years ago he'd discovered Boyd as a kitten under the porch of a house he'd been contracted to rebuild, and had brought him home. Since then Boyd had taken his place as one of Willie's dependents, giving little and taking much.

In the bedroom, Carmen was under the covers reading a book on Rembrandt. Willie got in beside her and leaned to see the page. Plate fifteen. *Self-Portrait* (1663). There was the great man himself, sixty years old, pulling no punches when it came to recording the puffy face, the dour expression, the dark-eyes, the sloping shoulders and long silver hair. She turned the page to a self-portrait done sixteen years earlier. The forty-four-year-old Rembrandt was a dandy, sporting an earring, a rakish cap, finely worked tunic, or jerkin, or whatever the hell it was called; his hair was dark, and his eyes were gazing not at the viewer but into the distance, because in those days he had a future.

What, Willie wondered, was *their* future? He'd made some significant strides toward reconciliation during the drive home. He'd made vows and promises and resorted to one of Rollo's pet phrases, reminding her that they had to "keep their eyes on the prize." One cliché after another presented itself to him: they had a good thing going, they'd come a long way, it was just a bad patch. He'd spoken with feeling, his eyes wet, wishing she could see that he was on the verge of tears, but she kept her gaze turned resolutely away, smoking cigarette after cigarette, not deigning to open the window, the smoke flowing along the ceiling and down the windshield to lay like mist on the dashboard. Willie's eyes stung. An urge to shout at her reared and then subsided. Finally, deciding he had suffered sufficiently, she did him the honour of resting her hand on his thigh.

His grovelling humiliated him, and now in bed, trying to regain some ground, he grew bold. "Kind of a coincidence," he observed.

"What a great book this is. What a perfect present, Willie. Thank you." She gazed at him with those velvety eyes and an admiring expression, as if he never failed to impress her with his thoughtfulness. He'd given her the book last year for her birthday. She tilted herself toward him and pecked him on the lips. "I can't help it if he was there when I walked in," she said. "What am I supposed to do, not sit with him?" Before Willie could respond, she was studying the book again. "It's our relationship with our self-image. It's about making them match." She lay the book face down in her lap and brought her palms together as if to pray. "Self and self-image. It's almost like yin and yang."

"You need another show," he said, strategically. Though she hadn't sold in her last show, she'd got a couple of good reviews in the local alternative press, including a rave in *Slam* that she cut out and carried in her wallet.

> Carmen Conway's new show *I for an I* at the Napalm Gallery explores the essence of what it means to be an individual in a relational world. Trumping the synthesizers with her unabashed attention to the topographical self and the landscape of the adamantine psyche, she directs us along a Möbius strip of mirrors in which, at every turn, at every loop, we meet we. It is a daring confrontation, the eye of the I. Her candour is refreshing, her draughtsmanship bold, her colour real, unreal, surreal. Runs to the end of the month.

As for a caustic little piece in *Bark* suggesting that while she was a competent draughtsman her navel lint was less than worthy of wall space, she'd written a vicious reply that earned her an even more caustic rebuttal. She ritually burned the review, and cursed the reviewer each full moon for the next three months, calling down upon him a plague of car crashes and beatings and a case of AIDS. Since then she'd been turned down by nearly every gallery in the city.

"I know I need another show," she said.

He reassured her. "It'll happen."

She stared harder at her book. "Things don't just happen. Not good things. Shit happens. I need a studio. What am I supposed to do, work in the bathroom?"

"I'll get you one. I'll get you two."

She became immeasurably sad. The corners of her mouth turned downward and she swallowed hard. "Don't patronize me, Willie."

"Hey. I'm not. You need a studio. I will get you one. I said I would and I will."

"Is there any steak left or did you guys scarf it all?"

Willie heard the accusation. "In the fridge."

She stepped out of bed and padded down the hall to the kitchen leaving Willie contemplating the word patronize. He liked to think of himself as a patron of the arts. He loved that she painted, he just didn't understand why she always had to paint herself. Why had she never wanted to paint him? Or the cat? Carmen returned a moment later, tearing at a slab of cold steak, followed by Boyd. Meat dangling between her teeth, Carmen got back under the covers. They could hear Boyd purring, gathering himself before he hopped up onto the bed and took his place at their feet. He regarded the meat that Carmen held in one hand while turning a page with the other. He waited hopefully for the next ten minutes until, concluding that his gifts of dead moles and sparrows had been wasted, he turned away.

Carmen slapped the book shut and suddenly announced out of the blue: "He's a little shit. Three thousand a month?

Some friend. With all you do for him?" She gazed at him, profoundly injured by the injustice. "He's a cold person, Willie. And that soul patch?" She shuddered. "I don't think it's going too far to say that Rollo and Angela — and believe me, Willie, I know it hurts to hear this — both of them are slightly psychotic."

To Willie, the word psychotic meant knife-wielding mad, and he thought that it was a tad strong in reference to his daughter.

She saw his scepticism. "Divorced from reality, Willie. That's the main symptom. At two with reality. You can't tell me that expecting three grand a month is realistic. That's blood from a stone. And I'm sorry but you can't tell me that Angela is any better. She's not seeing the world for what it is. She's a bright girl," she conceded. "And she's got so much potential." Carmen paused to contemplate the breathtaking enormity of Angela's untapped potential and the tragedy of how it was being squandered. "But she really needs a talking to."

"I try."

Carmen put her hand on his arm. "I know you try. You do everything for her. And she's young."

For a few moments they contemplated Angela's youth. Willie wondered when young became old enough to know better. He sighed. They needed a holiday. "Hey, Ed's going to Mexico."

"Ed?" Carmen's tone of incredulity summed up her opinion of him, and caused Willie a pang of indignation on old Ed's behalf. "Mexico. . . ." Carmen breathed the word as if tasting the sunshine and tequila. "We should go, too."

Willie performed some noises implying that it was not an utter impossibility.

Carmen rolled to face him, eager, kittenish. "We should, Willie. It'd be good for us. For our relationship. Look at the money you spend on Angela."

"She's twenty-four."

"I was married by twenty-three," said Carmen, her tone slightly less conciliatory.

"You're her stepmother," said Willie.

"My point exactly. Mythically it is a very tough role. I'm evil incarnate."

"She's my daughter."

"And you're robbing her of key growth passages. She will never gain the self-esteem achieved by independent problem solving."

Willie suspected Carmen was quoting some magazine article, but he also knew that she was right. "She hasn't mentioned this Gabriel guy to you, has she?"

"To *me*? Hardly. I wish she would. I've tried with her, Willie, I have. I try not to take it personally because I know she's young. Still, it's tough, it's painful, she's a hurtful person." She rolled away from him, the spaghetti strap of her burgundy slip straining across her frail shoulder, and she began to sob.

He watched and was aroused. He shifted closer — his groin nestling up against her bum — put his arm around her and gave her a reassuring hug. "Hey, I should get five hundred for this trim tomorrow. We'll go out for dinner. You and me. In a week we'll have sixty thousand dollars. Maybe more." He leaned closer and said it again, in a smooth and coaxing voice rich with all the possibilities of money. "Sixty grand. One week. Seven days."

"If we went to Mexico we could see Frida Kahlo's studio," she said.

He slid his arm down along her waist and up the slope of her hip and on down to her thigh; meeting no resistance, he snuggled even closer, letting her feel his arousal. How warm she was, how sleek the feel of her slip. Nice. This was how they should be. He placed a row of kisses like red roses all the way up the path from her shoulder to her neck and inhaled the scent of her hair. "Mexico," he said, "a room with a balcony, tropical plants, the sea, birds."

"Birds?"

"Lots of birds. Parrots, mynahs, toucans."

"I love toucans."

He slipped his hand between her thighs where it was warm and smooth and snug and they began to make love. The light was still on in the room and Willie spotted one of Carmen's self-portraits on the wall. In the picture her hair was pulled back so tightly she looked bald. A shadow falling across her face suggested a moustache. And then there was the expression in her eyes, as if she were watching, or spying. In the crow-hop of association, he recalled the bald man sitting in the Princeton pretending to read the racing form. Why was he looking at Willie? Why was he familiar? And why was Rollo there? Willie rolled away, mumbling apologies about too much beer and a headache while Carmen resumed weeping.

CHAPTER 9

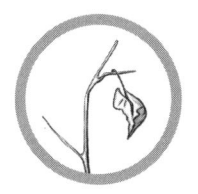

BY EIGHT IN THE MORNING Willie was speeding east on the freeway into the far suburbs: light industry giving way to industrial parks morphing into shopping malls merging into condos transforming seamlessly back into more malls. The commuters were fulfilling their functions in the Great Chain of Commerce. Caffeine-fevered creatures hunched hard over the steering wheels of identical Hondas and Datsuns and Nissans. Where were the cars of yesteryear, the '65 Mustang, the Barracuda, the Comet, the Corvair, the Valiant, the Bug? Gone. All gone. These new models were as generic as seal-and-burp plastic-ware. Was that a Hyundai or a Mercedes? Plastic hula girls swaying on dashboards raised embittered recollections of overpriced holidays on Maui, the hotel not four-star but two, the side-table drawers boiling with roaches, the locals surly, the cab drivers thieves, the cocktails weak, the *ahi ahi* mush, the exchange rate staggering. And now they were paying those holidays off, or trying to, a Sisyphean labour what with Visa and Mastercard charging nineteen percent interest. They geared up and changed lanes but the debts followed.

One unforeseen benefit of going into the marijuana business had been escaping this commute. In the mornings while tending the crop, Willie would sip a coffee and listen to the news and could not deny a tickle of glee at reports of volume delays on the Ironworkers Memorial Bridge, of a stall on the freeway, or that it was backed up on 99 South.

Shootings inspired by road rage did not surprise Willie; that there were so few did. And he could hardly blame anyone for quietly opting out of a career much less a job that required enduring such a spirit-poisoning commute. He did the arithmetic. An hour there and an hour back for, say, two hundred days was sixteen days a year. That was four hundred days over a thirty-year working life, or over one entire year spent sitting, fuming, frustrated, defeated, in traffic.

Willie reached to switch on the radio and then hesitated, fingers outstretched and trembling, aching for and yet dreading news of the latest death splatter. He gripped the steering wheel tighter, opting instead to drive in silence, while the Attar of Rose deodorizer dangling from his rear-view disseminated a chemical scent that raised visions of *houris*, except such sweet visions of the Mythic East were now tainted by the fireballs of exploding jetliners, glowering ayatollahs, and George W. Bush.

A '70s Ford pickup slid by him, fenders racketing, the body

blasted with corrosion. In the back stood a table saw and a battered tool chest. Willie had loved his tools. When he'd been forced to sell the business to pay off his debts he'd held onto his red metal tool chest with its three interior trays. He'd never sell his Japanese draw saws, his blue-steel planes or his Ryoguchi hammer. He'd used that hammer on so many jobs for so many years he could feel it in his hand even now like a phantom limb. Sloppy work insulted such crafted tools. Another reason he trimmed his crop with such precision.

Willie hated trimming bud for strangers, and he was indignant not only at taking the risk but also the drop in status of hiring himself out like this. He should have told Carmen she'd have to wait; they'd all have to wait. Yet while Willie knew exactly how much weight and strain a joist or post or main bearing wall could endure, he was timid about stressing human relationships. He didn't want to face the prospect of tearing something down and starting over. So, like a homeowner too cheap to demolish and build anew, Willie found himself resorting to what bad carpenters used, a substance known in the trade as "three-quarter inch putty." You covered up. You packed gaps and crevices and badly measured joints with putty and lies, slapped on some paint and hoped no one noticed. In both building and relationships this only delayed disaster. In his heart of hearts — that rarely visited closet deep inside — Willie suspected that most of his relationships were tear-downs.

*

Willie drove past the address, parked a block down the street and walked back, covertly studying the houses and cars. A neatly generic neighbourhood of Vancouver Specials. Then he saw the address and his heart clenched at the state of the house, a hold-out from the 1950s not unlike Rollo's, but in the furthest stages of disrepair: mismatched shingles, peeled and blistered paint, lawn running amok, blankets instead of curtains in the windows, while two sun-blistered reindeer drew a wooden Santa and sleigh through the dead juniper bushes in the scorched garden. They might as well have erected a neon sign. He considered turning around and getting back in his van and driving home. Instead he proceeded up the weed-grouted walk and up the steps where he saw that the bits of crushed glass sprayed onto the stucco on either side of the door had been picked away as though some sullen teen, some idle child, a bored or preoccupied man, had spent time on the porch, exiled or waiting, with nothing better to do, and the result was that the house looked as though it had mange. He rang the doorbell. The smell of boiled cabbage reached him as he waited. When the door finally opened a crack — the chain still secured — Willie saw an eye regarding him.

"Smell anything?"

"Cabbage."

As if that was the password, the guy smiled showing teeth so short they might have been filed. He opened the door just wide enough for Willie to slip in.

"Lance."

"Willie."

Lance wore mirrored shades, a Labatt Blue visor, and a *Count Me In! BC Census 2001* T-shirt. He led Willie through the kitchen and indicated the head of cabbage simmering in the enamelled stewing pot on the stove. The sink was a midden of dishes and the ancient Formica counters bubbled, the edging as wobbly as old chrome. Willie had been inside all of one minute and he knew the place intimately. He'd restored many like it, the house devolving through the decades from a modest but proudly maintained family home with waxed floors, painted window frames, a sturdy fence, and a well-trimmed lawn, to a rental house. From there it descended on down through the ranks to a young couple who might have briefly considered purchasing but didn't like the direction the neighbourhood was heading so left after a year; then a divorcee moved in but the alimony stopped and she vanished when her cheque bounced, this led to a group of students, and from there it was all over; an investor with an eye to the future bought it and in the meantime rented it to parolees and transients, anyone accustomed to live in squalor, at each stage the degradation hastening until the house was unsalvageable, fit only for the bulldozer or pot farmers.

Lance led him down the rickety basement stairs and showed him the crop.

"Are those horse cocks or are those horse cocks?"

"Some good-looking bud there," lied Willie, knowing that no matter how odd or ugly or stunted, praising a man's pot was as essential to harmony as praising his son. Yes, each plant had one donkey dick bulging with bud, but the lower quarters were bald, and that's where, with proper trimming and what Willie liked to call crop orchestration, you could up your yield by thirty percent. But cowboys like Lance, all they thought of was big bud, horse cock, which looked far more impressive than it was. The plants were six-foot Afghanis growing in dirt, and they stank like a troop of scared skunks. "How many?"

"Ninety-four." Lance grinned proudly. His teeth put Willie in mind of damp gyproc, chalky and grey. They were not only short but pitted, as if someone had experimented on them with a drill. Lance was about six-one, in his mid-fifties, and as lean as a down-pipe. He had shoulder-length grey hair, a long pointed beard and a hunch. Willie thought, put a wizard's cap on him and he could be Gandalf's wastrel brother. Willie didn't trust him. The sly look in the hard eyes bespoke a ratlike intelligence. Willie had no doubt that somewhere in this house lurked a stockless sawed-off shotgun, plenty of ammunition, and a variety of knives that even Daniel Boone would have feared.

"That's Rex," said Lance, introducing the other trimmers.

"Hey." Rex was a slim young Chinese guy in black jeans, singlet and cowboy hat.

"And that's Darrel."

Darrel was a lipless white guy with a small chin. He was Willie's age and wore a short-sleeved, button-down white shirt with a black bowtie poking up out of his breast pocket as though he ought to be managing a shoe department rather than trimming bud on a weekday morning. Darrel and Rex sat at a trestle table in black plastic patio chairs, working their way through a Captain Morgan's box full of rough-cut plants, and listening to the sweet sliding sounds of a violin concerto. The gentility of the music was both incongruous and somewhat reassuring. Willie drew out a chair and joined them.

"Don't mind Vivaldi, do you?" asked Lance, grinning his

grin. "The plants like the high notes. You know, light, happy, optimistic." Lance danced his fingers in the air as if conducting.

"Vivaldi's good," said Willie, more than a little bemused at finding himself trying to demonstrate his level of musical sophistication to Lance.

"Frankie Valli," said Darrel, sour-mouthed and grim.

Lance ignored Darrel's attempt at a pun. "Vinyl or acrylic?" Lance held out two boxes of surgical gloves. Willie chose acrylic, shook talc onto his hands then pulled on the gloves. Lance leaned on the table close enough for Willie to be tickled by the split ends of his beard. "Rollo says you trim lean. Me I prefer a looser style. I'm lookin' at a fast job here." He skated one palm off another. "One day. In and out."

"Fine by me." Willie wondered what else Rollo had said.

"Little salad's okay," Lance said amiably. He gave Willie a cardboard beer flat for his lap. "Catch the honey leaves. I'm trying to develop a market in honey leaves. Get a smoother buzz. A hippie buzz. Sell it to the kids on Wreck Beach."

The honey leaves were the leaves sprouting in and around the bud itself and they did indeed induce a tasty high. Willie momentarily considered bonding with Lance by remarking that he too collected them, but decided against it. *Don't tell 'em nothin' about nothin'.* He reached into the Captain Morgan's box and picked out a branch muscled with resinous green bud and, sliding his own pair of Japanese grapevine scissors from their plastic sheath, started in snipping away fan leaves.

Lance disappeared into the forest of Afghanis and Darrel resumed his conversation with young Rex. "Yeah, I'll take a Louisville Slugger to their shins. I'll bust their kneecaps. I'll pulp them. You ever see what a baseball bat does to bone?"

Rex did not look up from his trimming. "No, but I have a good imagination." Rex was about twenty-five, fit, clean. A Diet Coke and a pack of Dentyne sat by his elbow.

Darrel leaned toward him as if to impart a delicious detail, and whispered, "They'll have Kraft Dinner for legs." Hoping he'd caused a tremor of shock with his imagery, he nodded once, like punctuation at the end of a sentence.

Willie kept his gaze on the bud but listened intently.

Rex seemed at ease with Darrel's dramatics. He yawned and said, "You know him?"

"I'll find him. Believe me, I'll find him."

Willie cleared his throat. "You get poached?"

Darrel gave Willie the angry eye. "Fucker who trimmed for me. Had a barn show out in the valley. Hired four guys. One came back and paid me a little visit. Which is why my real name ain't Darrel, which is why I'm wearing what I'm wearing, which is why I grow small now and bring 'em down myself."

Willie looked to Lance who was grinning maliciously from amid the plants, looking less like a degenerate Gandalf now than a crazed survivalist plotting doom from the bush. Willie asked Lance, "How do you know Rollo?"

"Oh, I've known Rollo-boy a long time," said Lance, hinting an involved and gnarly history.

In all the years he'd known Rollo the guy had never mentioned Lance. Maybe Rollo was more circumspect than he'd given him credit for. It occurred to Willie he could mention seeing Rollo in the Princeton last night — to confirm Rollo's story about meeting Lance there — but he kept his mouth shut. They trimmed through the morning, listening to three news reports, the Four Seasons, some Chopin mazurkas, and a selection of Puccini arias sung by Cecilia Bartoli.

"Where's the washroom?" asked Willie.

Lance pointed to the stairs. "Up and right. Take your shoes off. Don't want leaves gettin' tracked around."

"Details," agreed Darrel, shaking his head as if he'd seen too many good men laid low by ignoring details like leaves.

Willie took his Nikes off and went up the rubber-lined steps, opened the door and entered the intestinal smell of cooked cabbage that masked the pong of the skunk. Great tongues of peeling paint were lolling from the bathroom walls. He peed and washed then searched for a clean spot on the grubby towel where he might dry his hands. Failing to find one, he reeled off a few yards of toilet paper and used it instead. Lack of sleep was catching up with him. He put the toilet lid down and sat for a few moments with his elbows on his knees and his head in his hands. All in all it wasn't going too badly, though by the looks of things he'd be lucky to come out with three hundred dollars. He would take Carmen out for supper tonight, get her some flowers, make love. Last night's failure in bed brought up a rush of embarrassment. How to explain the functioning — or more importantly the malfunctioning — of the penis to a woman? Maybe he should buy some pornography and keep it hidden so he could prime himself beforehand? How far he'd come from those testosterone teen years when he'd masturbate before seeing his girlfriend so as not to come too soon. He heard a fly battering itself against the scalloped window above the tub. He watched it for a moment, inclined to attribute existential characteristics to its dilemma. The fly fell still, perhaps in a moment of metaphysical acceptance of its lot. Willie had spent a lot of time noticing flies. Every house he ever rebuilt or upgraded was full of them, even in mid-winter. When the afternoon sun warmed a south-facing window it would soon stir with revivified flies; crank the heat on a house that had stood empty for a year and by noon the windows would fizz with the newly hatched. They always hovered at the window, as if they liked to take in the view, enjoyed the feel of sleek hard glass, or were drawn to the conundrum of something hard yet invisible to their five eyes. No one liked flies — not even kids who ate them and certainly not the boys who plucked their wings. So common in contrast to the ladybug with its shellacked red shell, so filthy next to the elegance of the butterfly, so dull and hairy compared to beetles and the armorial metalwork of their backs, so drudgelike against the honeybee. Flies were made to eat poo and batter themselves against windows or be locked up in bottles. An insect under a curse. A creature condemned for past-life misdeeds. While the more aesthetically pleasing and entomologically intriguing bugs were caught up in gently cupped hands and carried like small royalty to be puffed to freedom out of windows and doors, only the rolled newspaper awaited the fly. Or the fly swatter. It was not the ladybug swatter or the beetle swatter or the bumblebee swatter but the fly swatter. Willie stood up from the toilet seat and slid open the window above the tub and with one puff gusted the defeated fly to freedom.

Stepping toward the door he put his foot in a puddle, soaking his sock. He cursed and leaned against the wall and dabbed at his foot with toilet paper. Number One, he hated wet socks. Number Two, what exactly was that puddle? As he dried his foot he heard voices outside beneath the window — hushed voices. Willie stepped up onto the edge of the bathtub and listened at the scalloped green glass. Men. Men pushing through foliage; men trying to be quiet.

Cops? The lilt of the voices said no. Their tone said no. Everything said no. His breath was pumping and his galloping pulse made him dizzy. Warn Lance? He turned and at that moment heard the measured boot . . . boot . . . of a heel bashing at the kitchen door. That door opened onto the sundeck, which was just down the hall. Willie slid the bathroom window all the way open and peeked out. Bush. The sundeck was around the side and the pounding now included the sound of splintering wood. They were breaking through, they were almost in, and they were less than thirty feet away. Out beyond the trees the blue sky lay serene and distant. A flock of sparrows twittered past. Old Ed was probably sitting on his back steps sipping a coffee and smoking a cigarette and thinking of Mexico. The kitchen door whacked back against the wall and Willie felt the entire bathroom shudder. They were in! This realization worked like a cattle prod forcing Willie onto the window ledge. He was two stories up. He reached out, gripped the gutter, hooked an elbow over and swung free. The metal gutter sagged under the strain of his weight — sagged but held — and Willie offered a prayer of thanks to the virtues of metal, and to the tradesman for not having skimped on the nails. He got his other elbow up and hung there, wide eyes staring up the steeply sloping roof, the coarse asphalt shingles biting his fingers, grating the sensitive skin of his inner forearms. He strained. His legs pedalled the air. He tried groping his way higher and a shingle slid free like a card from a deck, skimmed past his face and slashed down through the trees behind him. He groaned. He hadn't done a chin-up in decades. He groaned again and this time hoisted himself high enough to get his knee up and over.

Finally he lay flat on the roof, heart thumping so hard he feared he'd have a stroke. Gradually his heart slowed and his breathing settled. The shingle was coarse against his cheek and he could smell the sap in the nearby poplars. The roof was pitched so that the planes formed a valley that opened onto the bush at the back but was concealed at the front and sides. Willie crouched in that valley as he heard shouts coming muted through one of the vent pipes. Then he heard a shot. He sucked air and stayed down on all fours, his elbows shaking. There was only the breeze carrying the sap smell of the forest that stretched away up the mountain toward the blue-blue sky in which, to his amazement, a kite was flying. Yes, a kite. Somewhere some child was flying a kite.

And then Willie realized he had diarrhea.

Fear. The primal urge to lighten the body and expedite flight. The realization that it was coming — inevitable, unavoidable — made him whimper. He looked around and tried to be strategic. He worked himself in a stiff-legged crab-walk down the slope toward the edge of the roof, thinking he might squat there and relieve himself, but the pitch was too steep, he'd end up in the bush, pants around his broken ankles, in his own mess. Willie's dignity, such as it was, could not accept this. Yet time was ticking and his sphincter was trembling. He needed something to cling to, something, anything, then he saw it: the chimney. In a final push for the summit, Willie climbed. No mountaineer knew greater relief or exaltation as when he reached the chimney, hugged it with one arm, worked his jeans down with the other and squatted. His bowels burst in a scalding gush. Only once did he look at the streak oozing tarlike down the roof. After that he directed his attention up into the sky where trees swayed, birds tumbled, white clouds rolled and that kite rode the air currents at the end of its string. For a long time he remained hugging the hot and gritty chimney. He might even have lost consciousness and dreamed that he was a boy in a field flying a kite that soared high above the patchwork land and its lowly inhabitants. Socks ruined by the burning asphalt shingles, he pulled them off and used them as toilet paper then hauled himself upright, the muscles in his back, calves and ankles united in a chorus of agony.

And then the front door opened and men hustled down the steps. Van doors slid open. There was curt conversation. Willie crawled up the slope, peered over and saw three men in balaclavas stowing fire axes and bulging green garbage bags into an Econoline van. Before climbing into the vehicle, one dragged off his Balaclava and shook the sweat from his face, and it was him, the guy, the bald man with the handlebar moustache who'd been eyeing Willie in the pub last night. He got into the van, which kicked out a spray of gravel that clattered across the sun-blistered Santa in the garden.

Willie waited a few more minutes then began working his way down to the eavestrough. One peek over told him he couldn't climb back in the way he'd come out. He crossed to the porch, sat with his legs dangling over, dropped to the deck and rolled and lay there on his back. Not only were his feet throbbing, the soles stung as if he'd been walking across fire. There, in the sky, immune and beautiful, was that kite. He sat up. The kitchen door was kicked in. Willie hobbled inside, the lino blessedly smooth and cool, and discovered that the pot of cabbage had boiled dry and was smoking and trembling on the element. He switched off the heat. The cabbage looked like a clump of brains. He proceeded along the hall to the basement door where he heard muted moans. He eased the door open. The first thing he noticed was that his Nikes were not at the foot of the stairs where he'd left them. The second thing was movement on the grey cement floor, and a spreading spill of red that put him in mind of paint, but it was not spilled paint and he knew it. He heard more moans and scuffling. Another urge to void himself rushed him into the washroom, where he sat on the toilet until his insides were reduced to a flayed inner tube. He washed his face in cold water then turned to deal with the basement.

His strained thighs trembled as he descended each step. Inch by inch, the scene presented itself: Lance slumped in a glassy red sheet of blood, his hair and beard smeared. Lance kept trying to rise but his feet kept sliding as if he were on ice. Rex and Darrel had been hastily wrapped with duct tape, and shoved against the cement wall where they sat tilted together as if they'd been snoozing on each other's shoulders. They strained and they blinked and there was snot coming out of Darrel's nose, a big bubble of snot in one nostril that expanded and then shrank as he breathed in and out.

Willie might well have backed his way slowly up the steps and fled if Lance had not seen him; they'd made eye contact, Lance's gaze clamping onto him in a death grip. Willie was barefoot and loathed the thought of Lance's blood oozing up between his toes. Where were his shoes? He turned to go back to the stairs and search, but the pig squeal warning that arose from Lance's throat brought him back.

"Lance. Don't worry. I'm just looking for my shoes." Even as he spoke he heard how ridiculous he sounded. *Don't worry? Just looking for my shoes?* He stepped carefully, disgustedly, onto the slick of Lance's blood, praying that he would not slip and fall in it, not now, not ever. Slowly he knelt, lowering himself to Lance's level; Lance did not smell good, no, not good at all. Peeling the tape from Lance's mouth released a pressurized groan that escaped in a spew of blood and saliva that spattered Willie's forearm. He fought not to wipe it off for fear of insulting him.

Conversation was not at its best. Willie fumbled and babbled while Lance rolled in the gluey blood, his hands like mitts and his tongue flopping like an amphibian. Rex and Darrel meanwhile each bore a kicked-in-the-nuts expression that required little explanation.

Lance breathed as if he'd been running. "You . . . you . . . you . . ." he panted.

Willie's fingers refused to cooperate and he had to fight them to free Lance from the rest of the tape. Searching for a cloth to wipe away the blood, he dashed up the steps three at a time and stood in the burnt cabbage stench of the kitchen until he spotted a roll of paper towels. He wiped at his forearm. In the freezer he found a bottle of Bols Vodka, a Soft Gel hot and cold compress, and a tray of ice cubes. Even as he grabbed these things part of him knew they'd suspect him. They'd demand to know how it was he happened to step out of the room just before the men broke in? They'd give little credit to the fact that he was still here, that he'd helped them, and that he was obviously freaked out, fucked up and barefoot. These thoughts made Willie halt. He stood in the kitchen — vodka in one hand, cold pack and ice tray in the other, paper towels under his arm, the frantic dance of his bloody footprints staining the floor — and considered the implications. Yes, he had a good argument in his defence. If he was in on the poach he'd have split with them and would be in the van right now, laughing and hooting and chugging Jack Daniels. That was obvious. Something told him to go, now, while he could, just slip out the front door and get in his vehicle and vanish. But he stayed. Not because it was the right thing to do but because he didn't want them after him, for that would only create an anxiety that would cripple and haunt him on and on through sleepless nights until they found him and beat him with axe handles.

Lance was on his hands and knees making barking noises when Willie returned. A most disturbing display. Brain damage?

"Lance . . . Lance!"

Lance swung his head like a drunken buffalo, strings of bloody drool swaying from his lower lip.

"Take a drink." Willie cranked the cap from the vodka and held it before his face. One of Lance's eyes was so swollen it resembled a split plum.

"Fuck me."

For an instant Willie thought this was some demented sexual urge caused by a blow to the skull. And God knows Lance might well have been so heavily into s&m that this was all but a tasty bit of foreplay. "Lance! Have a drink. Come on." He raised the bottle and carefully decanted vodka into his mouth past the carious ridge of his lower teeth. Lance's gullet jumped to life and he gulped, much of the vodka going up his nose and down over his chin and neck, but some of it making it down his throat with a mind-clearing burn. He dropped back heavily, congealed blood sucking loudly between his jeans and the cement floor, his good eye opening wider to take in the destruction around him. Willie followed his gaze, and saw for the first time that all the trimmed pot plus all the plants — except one standing lonely in the middle of the last table — were gone. Lance's gaze rolled to a wobbly stop on Willie's face and Willie — crouched before him with the vodka bottle, the ice pack and the paper towels — waited in terror for Lance's conclusion.

"I'm gonna fuckin' eat your liver." Then he passed out.

Willie untied Rex and Darrel and helped clean them up with vodka-soaked paper towels. Darrel seemed to have broken ribs. Willie crushed five Tylenol into a glass of vodka and held it for him as he drank. Rex's wrist was broken and he was bleeding from the ears. Willie dispensed five more Tylenols and vodka. An ice tray down Lance's back returned him to soggy consciousness. Willie then drove them all to Emergency, Lance breathing muddily, Darrel groaning as if constipated, and Rex in a traumatized silence. A few times Lance began to speak but choked on the blood and muck clogging his throat.

Had they forced him to swallow something unspeakable? Indulged a little recreational torture while the opportunity presented itself? Willie turned into the hospital parking lot and the speed bumps made all three of them cry out. He helped check them in and explained to the nurse they'd been mugged by bikers in the parking lot of a convenience store.

"And what about you, sir?" she'd asked, frowning at Willie's bare, bloody feet. Her name tag said Immaculata, and her brown skin complemented her starched white uniform.

Willie saw where she was looking. "Me, I'm fine no problem." He babbled and gestured as he backed his way out through the pneumatic doors then turned and ran. He calmed down only when he was back in the van and in the thick of the traffic.

The dashboard clock read 2:43 in the afternoon. They'd robbed them in the middle of the day. The boldness of it was breathtaking. One plant left standing. The same guys. Their trademark. The further Willie got from Lance's place the more he began noticing the aches throughout his body. It was as if the pains were not only becoming more intense but actually getting louder, as if they had volume — bass, treble and pitch — and more than once he moaned aloud. The soles of his feet burned, his fingertips felt as if they'd been whacked with hammers, his back was in spasm, his neck kinked, he'd banged his knees and shins, and even the muscles in his armpits — were there muscles in one's armpits? — ached as if he'd free-climbed a thousand-metre face. There was also blood — as pungent as wet pennies — all over the front and back seats. It was all too much for the Attar of Rose deodorizer. He pulled into a self-serve gas station and motored across to the air and water pumps and spent half an hour scrubbing. He balled up the rags and paper towels and shoved them into the bin then hurried into the washroom for a final rinse so that he did not arrive home looking as if he'd just slaughtered a goat. He scrubbed and dried his feet and wondered what that nurse must have thought of him, and if she'd called the police. Leaning on the sink, he stared into the mirror: close-set eyes, narrow head, weak chin, nondescript nose, oatmealish complexion. He leaned closer and tried to see his soul in his eyes, not as if peering into a mirror but through a window, at the distant figure of himself as a boy perhaps, wandering alone in a sunny field, but there were no fields in the East End, there were abandoned lots and railroad tracks, seagulls and freighters, and right now he was standing in a gas station toilet.

He pulled into the carport at exactly five o'clock, switched off the motor and sat listening to the ticking of cooling metal. He'd been having little success coming up with a scenario that would keep Carmen's panic in check and didn't feel any more inspired now that he was home. He got out and limped across the lawn past Ed's Winnebago with its golf course mural. What would Marcus Aurelius say about the situation? Forthright honesty or prudent lies? He climbed the steps to the porch on his wobbly legs and found Carmen and Rollo seated at the kitchen table.

"The fuck you do now?" demanded Rollo.

"Willie —" Carmen stood. Despite his efforts at cleaning himself up, she saw the state of him and was devastated. The depths of her concern pleased him. His woman cared, yes, she was eccentric and selfish, but she cared. She opened her arms to give him a hug, took a step toward him, then put her hands to her mouth and began to cry.

Needing the comfort and reassurance of her warm clean body, Willie embraced her and patted her back and made soothing sounds. "It's okay."

"You smell like blood." She pulled away, appalled. "And where are your shoes?"

For a moment he recalled all the times he'd lost his shoes as a kid and endured the wrath of his mother, but only for a moment. Slumping into the nearest chair he looked at Rollo. "Got poached."

"I know you got poached. Fuckin' Lance just called from Emergency. He thinks it was you." Rollo lurched up and began to pace. "He's wonderin' how the fuck come you just happen to step out two minutes before the door comes down."

Indignation burned as bitter as bile up Willie's throat. "He's an idiot," he declared, haughty, dismissive, even as he was turning to Carmen and asking, "Do we have any aspirin?"

Carmen went down the hall to the bathroom and returned with a bottle of codeine tablets, shook out four and then opened him a beer. When he'd washed them down, he asked Rollo the obvious question, the question Lance should be asking. "Why would I stick around and drive them to the hospital?"

The usually meticulous Rollo was unshaved and puffy-eyed, his shirt was out and his deck shoes unlaced. He shook his head and continued pacing from the sink to the table and back to the sink, his arms crossed tightly over a coved chest that no regimen of push-ups or pectoral work could broaden.

"My rep's on the line here. And what's this about them leaving one plant?"

Willie glanced at Carmen who began backing away. Hyperventilating, her voice began to crack up. "I told you. They followed you. They're probably out there right now!"

Rollo dropped to his knees as if the house were being strafed, crawled to the window and lifted the curtain and peeked out.

Surprising himself with his own calm, Willie slouched back in the kitchen chair, crossed his arms over his chest and coldly regarded Rollo down there on the floor. The codeine was already rising like a warm bath inside him, dulling the pain in his feet and ballasting his thinking. He doubted they were about to do two raids in one day, and it enraged him that Lance couldn't understand that instead of suspicion Willie deserved thanks. "Anyway, Lance doesn't know where we live. Rollo. Lance doesn't know where we live, does he? Rollo?"

Rollo let the curtain slat drop and looked guiltily at Willie. "You wanted the gig; he needed a guarantee."

Carmen sucked a death-rattle breath and fell against the counter in a fit of uncontrollable trembling.

"I'm the one who drove him to Emergency! Why would I have done that? Why would I have stuck around?"

"I have to get out of here." The plaintive despair in Carmen's voice bespoke massive injustice: she didn't deserve this, she was innocent, she was a victim. Willie caught her as she fled past him for the door. Squirming in his arms, she suddenly went still and her eyes wide. "Give it to him. Give him the crop. He lost his — you give him yours."

Sacrifice his babies? Give up twenty-five pounds of green gold worth sixty maybe sixty-five or, who knew, even seventy thousand dollars? That was asking him to lose two crops in a row, that was asking him to admit defeat. If he lost this one it was all over, he wouldn't have enough money to float him through a third try, and he certainly wouldn't have enough money to be forking out for tuitions, rents and Mexican vacations. Where would that leave them? Broke and broken, is where. Without money he was powerless. Without money he'd never see Angela again, Juliet would drift away, and as for Carmen, well, he was afraid to put her to such a test. No. Ask him for a limb, ask him for an eye, but not his crop. He slowly shook his head.

"It's fair, Willie, it's fair."

Willie was in tears. Fair? Fair was working hard and getting paid. Fair was people who appreciated what you did for them. "That's my crop. That's our crop."

Carmen shook herself free. She straightened the hem of her shirt and spoke with dignity. "I'm going to a hotel. I will get a cab and I will go to a hotel. The Hyatt. I will go to the Hyatt." She nodded. "Therefore I need money, Willie, I need money." When he merely stood there in slack-shouldered impotence, gazing at her with sad eyes, she became hysterical. "Don't you see? Don't you comprehend what is going on here?" She gripped his shirt and spoke as if he was deaf and slow. "I am in danger. I need money!"

Willie gently held her shoulders and whispered: "I don't have any money, baby."

Her eyes hardened. "Sell the dope, Willie, sell the dope.

Get some cash and let's get out of here! Now! You and me. The two of us."

Willie looked at Rollo who was still down on his hands and knees by the window. The expression on Rollo's face suggested too many things for Willie to tweeze apart and analyze separately, but they included a strange look of betrayal and pain as he watched Carmen. "Call Lars," said Willie. "We'll bag the stuff right now and move it tonight."

⌒

Rollo flipped his cell shut. "Lars is on. But he wants more money. A lot more. Five thou."

"It's supposed to be one," said Willie.

Rollo shrugged. "Smells emergency."

"We need more wine," muttered Carmen, stabbing furiously at the Gala Keg with a carving knife to get at the last drops.

It occurred to Willie that Rollo was lying in hopes of pocketing the difference. "Maybe if I talk to him."

Rollo shook his head. "Not cool, not cool. Guy's major paranoid." Now Rollo became reasonable and his tone reflective. "He'll do five years if he gets nabbed."

Willie had in fact always considered Lars a chump for asking only a thousand when you considered the risk. Since 9/11 security had gone crazy, including teams of border vigilantes and motion detection devices. On the other hand, it was twenty minutes work, and it wasn't *Midnight Express* where you were going through customs under lights and cameras, and having to out-cool and out-think ravenous men hungry for your innocent flesh. No, it was just a matter of slinging on a pack and trotting across a field and into the trees.

Rollo tapped his fingers on the tabletop like a clock ticking down and watched Willie. Carmen shook the last splash of the wine into her glass, her red eyes pouched and swollen and her expression blanched with fear. Her beluga forehead was exposed because her hair was stuck to her temples with perspiration. She closed her eyes and gulped back the wine as if it were cyanide and she was eager for escape; when she opened them she looked at Willie as if he were the first creature she was meeting in the afterworld, an expression of fear and hope, for it was his call, he was the hub, the centre, the sun around whom they revolved. Rollo's fingers kept ticking off the seconds.

"No way, I'll do it myself."

CHAPTER 10

WILLIE GOT ONTO HIGHWAY 99 SOUTH for the border and was soon streaking through Richmond and then Surrey, the occasional hawk perched like a sentinel of doom on a fence post as he passed through the darkened farmland. The van still reeked of blood, a richly nauseating smell, like a pudding concocted of organ meat, the sort of savoury he imagined old Ed smacking his lips over. Willie cracked the window and air screamed past his left ear.

Willie and Rollo had done a hasty job de-stemming and weighing out the damp pot into twenty-five single-pound Ziplocs that Willie shoved into a backpack, which now sat in the back of the van under a blanket. Rollo had jabbered non-stop advice: "Wear dark clothes and a hat, and keep low to the ground, man. Real low. Like under the radar. And you gotta listen, right, 'cause there's always something, a car door or a cough. And don't think. You think, you're fucked. Just go. Like football. Hit that hole and go for green." The idea was that Willie park then hike toward the border, orient himself via two stop signs Rollo sketched on a square of paper, then walk through the fields and the scrub cottonwood until he came to a waist-high string. He'd follow the string to the right and leave the stuff at the base of the tree it was tied to. That was it. Turn around and don't look back. A call would come to Rollo in the morning stating where and when to meet. In a day or two they'd have the cash and Lars could piss up a rope.

Carmen had recommended Willie take his passport, and Rollo agreed, saying that without it they'd stick him in jail no questions asked even if he was clean and minding his own business. Willie didn't want to think in those terms, but took their advice and buttoned his passport into his shirt pocket.

He stayed in the right-hand lane and kept the speedometer at ninety kliks. The cars in the fast lane slid past and Willie envied every one of those mundane, mediocre, routine lives. He saw silhouettes in Subarus and Fords, vans and SUVs. It was 12:45 Saturday morning. Everyone heading home from parties and movies to make love, to sleep late, and maybe have breakfast in bed. Willie rolled the window down all the way and the air rushing in carried the smells of farmland, a fresh fecund scent of ripe earth in the cool summer night. He'd heard on the radio that the Perseid meteors were already visible; squinting up through the windshield at the sky he saw nothing.

Willie took the turnoff, and all too soon had parked on the

side of the road and was faced with the task at hand. This was it. He took deep breaths as if priming himself for a plunge in the icy ocean. What if the string was not there, or he couldn't find it, and how was it that this string hadn't been discovered by the border patrol? He considered phoning Rollo for answers but what was the point? He kept the van running, to reassure himself that he'd be back in mere minutes, because of course he would be back in minutes. He would. And by leaving the ignition on he could claim he'd just stepped into the bush for a pee if some cop happened to come along. A few minutes from now, half an hour tops, he'd be on the road home, the job done, his anguish over; he'd turn the radio on and enjoy a leisurely cruise back into town.

He reached and pulled the pack from beneath the blanket and held it in his lap. Twenty-five pounds of pot, seventy-five thousand dollars, cash, tax-free. He glanced around one last time, opened the door and got out, pressed it quietly shut and pulled the backpack on. His guts churned as if he were digesting crushed glass. The motor idling contentedly, he began walking.

The sky was clear and the night balmy with the scent of clover and sap. Ten more crops, two years, and he'd have that orchard, or maybe only a year and a half or even less, fifteen months. Then it would be time to go orchard shopping, or head for Mexico. Maybe that wasn't such a bad idea, they could live years on the cash. As he walked, the low rumble of the idling van faded and then merged into the distant sounds of trucks and crickets and midnight industry. He could smell the low-tide sea less than half a mile away to his right. He wore jeans, a black sweatshirt, and a dark blue baseball cap. He reached a road and crouched in a deep dry ditch. On the far side was a stretch of waist-high grass and then a line of cottonwoods. Somewhere in that bush was the border, the 49th parallel, on this side good-hearted Canada (a country with a leaf on its flag couldn't be all bad), and on the other the imperialist U.S. beast. He thought again of the border patrols, avid men in army fatigues creeping about in the bush wearing night-vision goggles and equipped with shotgun mikes sensitive enough to catch a cat. He didn't want to think about that. Rollo said avoid any paths because they were rigged with motion detectors. A car approached. Willie stretched out in the bottom of the ditch with his face in the bitter weeds. The motor noise rushed toward him — the driver's foot to the floor — and Willie heard the whoops of joy-riding teens and the shatter of a flung bottle bursting on the rocky roadside. He waited a few moments, then raised his head like a groundhog scenting the air and watched the tail lights fade, leaving nothing but wind and the faint crackle of power lines. His back was soaked with sweat beneath the pack, which belonged to Angela, who had dumped it at Willie's along with so much else of her accumulated junk.

Keeping low, he followed the ditch to the T-junction and the stop signs and and hunkered down, his shadow resembling a hunchbacked troll emerging from beneath its bridge. He looked around, and to the east, rising above the trees, saw the moon, full and round and as brilliant as a searchlight aimed straight at him and him alone. The contours of stones and weeds at the upper edge of the ditch took shape in the new and unwelcome light.

Right now Rollo was alone with Carmen . . . Rollo lusted after her. He had lusted after Mercedes as well, but the insecticide of her disdain had kept him back. *If I just went back to the van and drove home? Would I catch them?* Rollo owned two houses and a sailboat and he liked to party and he loved Mexico. *You're a putz, Willie. Rollo is home consoling your woman while you lie in a ditch. Catch them or not catch them, it doesn't matter, but go home, go to bed, save your ass, now!*

But he would never be able to go to bed again, not in that house, not with Lance after him, and Lance would be after him, Lance was probably thinking of Willie right now, and if the painkillers had finally conked him out, he was probably dreaming of him and the glorious vengeance he would take. Hand over the crop? Then what? Angela's visits would be replaced by phone calls and her phone calls would grow less and less regular; unable to pay the rent, Rollo would turf him, he and Carmen would be on the street, and that meant that the tensile strength of Carmen's love would finally be tested. *Get back in the van. It's time to find out where all these people really stand.*

He held his breath, listened, then climbed out of the ditch as if going over the top at the Battle of the Somme, running in a crouch and squinting in the dark against the tall grass whipping his face, expecting any moment the shouts of Drug Enforcement agents to hit him like shots. Yet it wasn't a shot or a shout that stopped him, but stepping into a hole and twisting his ankle. With a groan he flopped onto his face, and, groaning through clenched teeth, rolled side-to-side cradling his foot. In an icy sweat, he shivered and thought he might vomit, while in a small clear corner of his brain he pined nostalgic for the warm dry security of his ditch. As he lay there his imagination searched around and settled on the worst-case scenario: gleeful DEA agents behind snarling dogs finding him scraping pathetically at the dirt trying to bury his cargo of dope. They surround him and stand there laughing their huge, hearty, meat-fed laughs. They give the dogs enough leash to tear at his clothes and soak him in rabid saliva. They nudge him with their boots, perhaps pretend to stumble over him, kick him in the ribs, and then apologize, calling him sir as they do so.

Instead, the moon continued to rise and the pain slowly abated and the night sounds — the crackle of wires and the gearing down of trucks approaching the border — resumed. He sat up, the twenty-five pound pack feeling more like two hundred, and tentatively moved his ankle, which kick-started the pain. His throat was dry and he was thirsty. He got up and started off once more, each step piercing his injured ankle with poison. When he reached the cottonwoods and the smell of sap and mulch, he realized he'd lost his alignment with the two signs on the road. He halted and looked back. Return? Start over? If he did he'd just get into the van and head home. He squinted at the stars through the web-work of trees as if that might orient him, felt useless, whimpered a little, then crept deeper into the bush, feeling for the line that would lead him to the tree where he could leave the pot and then escape. The rising moon was swiftly transforming the bush into a phantasmagoria of shadows. Both arms shielding his face, he advanced against branches that bumped and stroked and prodded. And then he heard breathing, breathing that was getting louder. His own, or had he come upon a young couple humping? But the breathing was getting closer, and faster, and accompanied by footsteps crunching twigs. He crouched. A shape bowled past so close he could have reached out and grabbed it by the ankle. A ghost? Some wraith lost in a half-world that briefly intersected Willie's? The beams of frantic flashlights began striping the tree trunks and a mega-phoned voice rang out: "This is the U.S. Drug Enforcement — Hey! Hey! *Hey, you motherfucker!*" Huddled on his hands and knees, Willie heard the thrashing-thumping-cursing of a clumsy pursuit. He forced himself to wait where he was until the noise passed on by and retreated into the distance, and then he burst like a rabbit from its hole running in the opposite direction. When he broke from trees to grass he dropped into a crouch so low his thighs thumped his chest at each step and he continued until he pitched into the welcoming ditch and landed on his back, the rucksack full of marijuana cushioning the landing. By now the twenty-five single-pound bags had been shaken into the shape of a lumpy pillow. He lay panting at the stars blurred by the sweat burning his eyes, while in the distance he heard shouts, a crackle of radios, a bark of laughter. The moon crested the rim of the ditch and grinned down at him as if finding entertainment in the mad antics of Willie LeMat. Car doors closed, engines started and then tires crunched slowly across gravel, which transformed into a smooth acceleration as the vehicles reached tarmac.

Willie sat up and looked around. Something was wrong. This was not his ditch, this was not his ditch at all, it was an American ditch, he knew the difference by instinct, the way you know you're being watched or that the phone is going to ring, or that the photo you are looking at is of a sunset and not a sunrise. He'd run the wrong way. He found a rusted license plate, picked it up and wiped at the dirt: WASHINGTON. There indeed was George's bewigged silhouette.

He estimated he was about a mile east of the Pacific Border Crossing. Hop a bus back into Canada? No one would expect him to be taking pot *into* his home and native land. Willie looked again at the bush from which he'd emerged. Hike back? Maybe the agents wouldn't be expecting two runs in one night. He imagined a narc after his shift was done, unstrapping his belt and prying off his boots in the living room of his mortgaged, double-wide trailer, a tale to tell the wife and son — *then Daddy stomped him, got that dirty dope dealer in a full nelson, and you know what I said to him, I said, boy: you're mine. That's when he wet himself, just went all melty in my arms. And he began to cry. Snivelled like a baby, and called on the good Lord. They do that. I've seen it before. Because you see, son, these are the wretched of the earth, and they crawl on their bellies, and yet for all that they are loathsome they do desire in their heart of hearts to be redeemed. . . .* Willie turned from the bush and looked at the road. If he could reach a phone booth he could call Rollo and tell him to come get him, or hook Willie up with the contact and salvage the deal.

The moon was floating high overhead now. Willie spent the next half hour listening, scanning for signs, lights, voices, anything that would betray the presence of narcs, but the more he studied the bush the more it twitched and swayed. And then a cop car appeared, turned right along a gravel road, dust swirling in the taillights, and disappeared into the bush.

Tarmac hard under his heels, Willie crossed the road and, trying not to limp, held his head high and relaxed as he walked along, just a guy out for a stroll under the silvery moon . . .

Fifteen minutes down the road he passed the entrance to a trailer court. On an archway of logs hung a sign carved with the name Mira Del Mar. A little further on he heard a vehicle, glanced back and saw a pickup emerging from the trailer court. Soon it was next to him. The driver's arm lolled out the window with a lit cigarette dangling in his fingers. He drove very slowly and as he passed Willie the man looked over, big and beefy and wearing a baseball cap and glasses.

"Nice night."

"It is," agreed Willie in as cheerful a voice as he could muster.

The man gestured with the cigarette. "Givin' the pooch its exercise."

Willie saw a dog tied to the trailer hitch, its paws pattering the pavement. "Good."

"Hittin' the road, are you?" he said, indicating Willie's backpack.

He could mutter something vague and keep walking, he could announce that he'd lost his job and his wife and was looking for work, he could say he was heading for the Copper Canyon in Mexico, he could even ask the man for a ride. Instead, inspired, he asked, "You couldn't let me have twenty dollars, could you?"

The man's bonhomie vanished and he geared up, forcing the dog to trot faster so as not to be dragged. As it passed him, the dog rolled its eyes at Willie as if appealing for help.

The scent of apples told Willie that he was next to an orchard. He climbed down into the ditch and up the other side. Suddenly desperate with thirst, he picked a few blackberries and almost wept at their sweetness. Oh for those simple summer days of picking the blackberries behind the gas station. He unslung the pack and, using it as a shield, forced his way through the thorny vines to the wire fence, paused to listen — heard only the simmering of insects — and so dropped the pack over and climbed after it and then stood in knee-deep grass beneath a tree jewelled with fruit. Apple trees. Everywhere. He looked for the beehives; fruit farmers always kept bees for pollination, but this orchard seemed to have been left to run itself into the ground. He spotted a stack of crates. The bees would be resting this time of night, but if there were any inside there'd be noise, the nocturnal hum of them dreaming of fields of flowering clover. He approached and listened. Nothing. He lifted a crate and shook the old combs and dead bees onto the grass. They were fragrant with the mulchy scent of raw honey, a mix of field grass and apple wood and small, dry, nectar-fed corpses. He distributed the pound bags into the crates and then restacked them. He felt buoyant, freed from the weight of the pack, and he rolled his shoulders. Angling his watch to the moonlight he saw the time was 3:21 a.m. Off through the trees stood a small barn, black and leaning as if bent by decades of wind, and beyond it was a house with a light burning. Could this be Ed's niece's place? The young widow? Was she awake, mourning her husband? Willie imagined a woman still young, wandering the empty house, drunk, talking to the spirit of the man she loved, and felt forlorn. An overwhelming urge to shut his eyes and forget everything overcame Willie. He sat down cross-legged in the grass and set the timer on his watch for 3:30, then lay back, groaning, the earth solid beneath him, and the tree limbs branching above while beyond them the stucco stars glinted. When was the last time he'd laid down on his back in an orchard? That would be the summer he'd picked apples in the Okanagan Valley, the summer he lost his virginity with Anne Pendleton from Calgary, his summer of love. He shut his eyes and recalled Anne's apple-scented hair, her inexplicable interest in him, and his breathless buoyancy at the sight of her. Willie was fifteen, and over his mother's objections had hitchhiked up from Vancouver. The pickers slept in tents or under the stars with the fallen fruit fermenting around them in the grass. How big his world had become; how tangible he suddenly was; and how perfect that their sleeping bags zipped together. All day they worked side-by-side, and at dusk the pickers ate at benches by the ranch house: apple pancakes, apple fritters, apple muffins, pork and applesauce, apple dumplings, apple cake, apple pie, apple ice cream and apple cider, vats of apple cider, and then the taste of apple on Anne's lips.

He woke to the metallic peep peep of his watch and sat up, ankle throbbing, throat parched, haggard and forlorn, even as he assured himself the worst was over, for after all he'd got the pot across the border. He'd succeeded, sort of. . . . He peered around, checked the dope one last time, then pushed his way back through the wire and blackberries to the ditch, and stood on the roadside trying to orient himself for when he returned for the stuff. Off to his right, maybe a mile away, were the lights of Blaine, the border town of porn theatres, cheap gas, and the stink of low-tide mud. He tucked his shirt in and started walking.

Half an hour later he entered a Denny's where he stood by the PLEASE WAIT TO BE SEATED sign hoping he didn't look as grubby and suspicious as he felt. Four in the morning and the place was purring with low-level laughter and the clatter of café cutlery, truckers and travellers chowing down over bowls of chili and hamburger platters. The smiling hostess arrived. She was large-eyed, round-figured and pretty, and her name tag said Lupe.

"How you tonight?"

"Great." Willie smiled and felt the sweat-crusted dirt cracking on his face.

Apparently used to all manner of nocturnal character, Lupe merely nodded as if genuinely pleased to hear that. "Bar or booth?"

"Booth."

She led him down an aisle between booths of orange and purple vinyl to a corner.

"Coffee?"

"Please. And water."

She heard the desperation in his tone. "Long night?"

He nodded.

She smiled in commiseration and her eyes flicked around indicating the crowded restaurant. "Tell me about it." She left the menu, a large-sized, multi-coloured, laminated fold-out that reminded Willie of a children's book, the sort he used to buy for Angela. He went to the washroom and in the mirror above the sink discovered that his face looked like he'd been whipped with razor wire and his hair pomaded with cow dung. Had anyone guessed his occupation from the state of his T-shirt and jeans they would have suggested gravedigger or sewer worker. Night shift on the road crew is what he'd tell Lupe. As he went at himself with the soap and hot water, assorted aches caught up with him: not just his ankle and calves, but a charley horse in his right thigh, a kinked neck, general all-over bruising, injuries he hadn't noticed, but which now stomped around inside him demanding attention: dull pains, sharp pains, pains that throbbed and pressed and pulsed, low level aches, scrapes and general stiffness. He would have liked to ask some of them to wait outside, or come back next month, or better yet try someone else altogether, because there was simply not enough room in his body to accommodate them all.

By the washroom door he dredged change from his pocket, read the long distance instructions, fumbled coins into the slot then punched Rollo's number. As the phone rang he checked his watch. 4:51 a.m. After four rings the answering machine clicked in: "*You've reached Rockin' Rollo and the All-Stars. Leave a message.*"

Though a glass door separated him from the rest of the customers, Willie shielded the phone with his hand and hissed, "Rollo! Rollo! It's Willie! *Willie!* Pick up!" But Rollo didn't pick up. Willie put more money in and redialled. Nothing. He called Carmen. No answer. He retrieved his change and called again. Still no answer. He considered the quarters in his hand,

George Washington's head on one side, an eagle's on the other. Maybe Carmen was too panicked to stay there alone. So where was she? Where was Rollo? They were together is where. He put his palm against the wall and leaned there.

Willie returned to his purple booth but couldn't finish his coffee because the caffeine hit him like strychnine, strangling his intestines. He drank his water and when the lovely Lupe returned he asked for a glass of milk, warm milk. His body was seizing up as tight as a rusted hinge. Even the movement involved in breathing made him hurt, his ribs themselves a barbed-wire hair shirt. Still, if he didn't keep moving he'd soon be all but paralysed. He drank his milk and, suppressing a groan, levered himself out of the booth, left Lupe a generous tip, briefly entertained a scenario in which she invited him home, nursed him, loved him, and, while he lay with his head in her lap, told him of her humble village in southern Mexico, how she missed the sound of roosters in the morning and the breeze in the palms. . . . He boarded the 6 a.m. bus for Vancouver, got off in White Rock, just over the border, used the last of his money to buy a can of gas because his van, unless it had been stolen, would have run dry, then he hiked three hours along the highway past bottles and chip bags and underwear and strips of truck tire, shifting his can of gas from hand to hand, and finally spotted his van waiting as faithfully as a dog.

CHAPTER 11

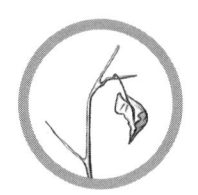

IT WAS NOON WHEN Willie got home. He didn't go right in but circled the block a couple of times studying the house for any suspicious signs, eyeing every vehicle in the area before finally pulling into the carport and cutting the motor. The first thing he noticed was that Ed's Winnebago was gone. He hadn't had a chance to say goodbye. No doubt, being Ed, he'd got an early start, which meant they might actually have passed each other at the border. With the Winnebago gone, a patch of bare dirt and pale withered grass lay exposed like a raw wound. Willie braced himself for the back spasms he knew were waiting for him when he tried to get out of the vehicle. He delayed the pain by taking his cellphone from the glovebox and punching Rollo's number.

He answered on the second ring and as usual got in the first hit. "Jesus Christ where the fuck you been?"

"Me? Where've *you* been?" said Willie.

"Here."

"I called you twice. I left messages."

"I didn't get 'em."

"The phone rang."

"I didn't get 'em."

"Where's Carmen?"

"What happened?"

"Where's Carmen?"

"I took her to a hotel."

"What hotel?"

"The Johnny Canuck."

"How come your phone works now?"

"What happened?"

Willie told him. "You gotta call the guy."

"No," countered Rollo, "*you* gotta meet me at that donut place on the corner of 33rd."

"Rollo —"

Rollo managed to click off before Willie did. Willie got the number of the Johnny Canuck from directory assistance and reached a woman at the desk who said there was no Carmen Conway registered and no Rollo Burgess, either now or last night. Willie decided that they'd used an alias. Something cute? Mr. and Mrs. Rollo Sexsmith? Studman? Cocker? Did they grope each other in the elevator, throw themselves onto the bed? He yanked the Attar of Rose deodorizer, a $1.39 gift from Carmen, off the rear-view and crushed it, its once sweet scent tainting his hand like some strange insect. Holding onto the steering wheel, he shut his eyes in preparation for pain and swore at the spasm clawing his back as he groped his way out of the van. Thighs trembling, he crossed the lawn then held the handrail as he mounted the steps to the back porch where he discovered the door ajar.

"Carmen?"

He stood in the middle of the kitchen listening carefully. It felt like weeks since he'd been here. "Carmen?" He stepped on through to the hall leading to the bedroom. "Carmen?"

The kitchen door shut behind him. Willie turned. A bald man with a handlebar moustache stood watching him, the man's tight T-shirt contouring a torso bulked in muscle. He stood with his back to the kitchen door, arms crossed like some malicious djinn rubbed from a bottle, a grin of infinite evil exposing tainted teeth capped with gold. A week's whiskers edged his jaw whereas his head was as smooth and shiny as if he'd shaved and waxed it that morning. The way he inclined his head to one side and appraised Willie suggested that they knew each other, and that Willie, sly, clever, incorrigible Willie, was up to his old tricks.

"You look like hell," said the man in a voice that had a faint formality to it, and the hint of a middle European accent, Hungarian or Serb, a man from the lands that, for so long, had buffered Europe against Attila the Hun, the Mongol hordes and the dreaded Turk. Willie thought of the decapitated head of cabbage boiling at Lance's place. He thought of heads on pikes displayed at the city gate. He was afraid.

Willie heard himself respond. "I feel like hell."

The man seemed to enjoy that. Yes, a little repartee. Such a variety of people he met in his line of work, not like those summers in the beet fields or the years in the Yugo factory. His mouth opened in a silent laugh exposing more gold. Then he stopped laughing and grew concerned. "She's good. But she's crazy." The man saw by Willie's expression that he didn't follow. "Her. The artist." He thrust his chin indicating Carmen's triptych above the kitchen table. There they were, three Carmens gazing out from the wall, bold of line and subtle of expression. Now the man pointed with his entire arm toward the living room. "She is everywhere," he said, appalled, as if Willie was at fault for allowing indulgence to be carried to such extremes. Did he not control his woman? Was he not a man? "And people," he asked. "Do they buy them, these pictures?" He was genuinely curious, willing to concede that if they made money, if people wanted them then they were, perhaps, excusable.

"No."

"No?" He frowned, the corners of his mouth turning downward. "Carmen Conway," he said, having apparently read the signature in the lower right hand corner of each work. "So she is not famous. She does not make a living. She is just crazy woman who sits before mirror with pencil." The man placed his palm over his heart. "And you, you love her so much you say, 'Please my dear, my darling, my love, keep painting, for I can never see enough of you.' And you hang them on the walls. Soon you will have to make new walls, new rooms, maybe stick them to the ceiling." He grinned, pleased with the absurdity of the madness.

Never had the extent of Carmen's self obsession struck him

with such blunt force. Before Willie was required to respond, footsteps thumped up the basement stairs and a woman of about thirty joined them. She was big, five-foot-ten and 180 pounds, with broad hips and a wide face. Her lichen-brown hair hung loose to her shoulders, she wore a Toronto Blue Jays jersey, and she gripped a baseball bat as lightly as a spatula. Her gaze cut from the bald man to Willie and back to the bald man, seeking her cue.

The bald man made a gesture of calm.

"How did you know?" asked Willie, surprising himself with his boldness.

The bald man raised his chin and mused as if it was not an unreasonable question. "You went to the same hydroponics shop once too often, my friend." He smiled almost sadly, not unappreciative of the labour Willie had put into his crop and the unfairness of him swooping in like a falcon to tear it from him. "I followed you."

The woman with the baseball bat shook her head and went *tsk, tsk.* "Details," she said in a melodious voice, throaty and sensual.

"The older growers are always the best," reflected the bald one. "They have patience. They grow good pot." He raised his hand and kissed his bunched fingertips as if speaking of wine.

The toilet flushed and a lean young kid of about twenty joined them, a dandy, groomed like a rooster, with black hair frosted blond at the tips, clean-shaven, sporting red leather driving gloves, black Levis and a red muscle shirt revealing hard round biceps surprisingly free of tattoos.

"Myron," said the older man. "We have company."

Myron regarded Willie with contempt.

Now the bald man walked straight at Willie, backing him into the hall where he stood trapped. "Where's the crop, my friend?"

"Gone. Sold."

"Sold? Then give me the money. Give me the money and we will leave you in peace to contemplate your pictures."

Anguish reducing Willie to a breathless wraith, he whispered, "I haven't been paid yet."

The bald man sighed, exhaling a puff of air as if he'd been through this sort of scenario all too often and it was becoming tiresome. The others adjusted their stances, the woman readying her baseball bat, Myron flexing his hands in his driving gloves. "Turn."

Willie turned and faced the wall where one of Carmen's pen and ink self-portraits hung. He was inches from her eyes. Her pupils were crosshatched. How humiliating to have his woman, even if it was only her sketch, witness this. His elbows were promptly seized and wrenched in one sure jerk up behind his back. Willie shouted and stood high on his tiptoes. The man's grip was terrifying. He held Willie by the triceps and began remorselessly squeezing his elbows together until they met in the middle of his back like folded wings, the fronts of his shoulders feeling as if they were about to split. He arched his back to ease the agony but the man, exhaling with the effort, now hoisted him right off the floor so that Willie's nose was rammed flat against the ceiling.

"We try again. Where's the crop, my friend?"

Willie's jaw ground soundlessly against the gyproc while

pain blazed white in his mind and he was certain his shoulders were dislocated. He could smell the man's briny stench, as if the effort required to hoist Willie aloft contracted not only his muscles but his sweat glands. The only response Willie could manage was a cry. The man dropped him. Willie landed on his hands and knees at the feet of the other two who stepped away as if he was a splatter of filth. He slumped helplessly, forehead on the floor, blood in his mouth, as hands slapped and tugged him and found his wallet and cellphone. Cards and papers hit the hardwood and his phone was kicked down the hall like a hockey puck. Among the papers were snapshots of Angela and Carmen.

"Nothing," said the kid called Myron.

"No plastic?"

"Nope." Then he added. "A passport."

"A passport? Farm boy is planning a trip." He slotted the passport back into Willie's shirt pocket. "Bon voyage. Put everything back," he told Myron, who scooped up the contents of Willie's wallet and gave it to the man, who contemplated it as though it was a deck of cards containing more jokers than aces. "But no credit cards."

"The bank took them," said Willie.

The woman with the bat let fly with a kick that would have crushed Willie's sternum had it not halted an inch before his chest. Instead of kicking him she gave him a nudge with her toe, a toe encased in a very familiar pair of Nikes, then laughed in that musical voice of hers.

Curled in the fetal position, Willie watched the bald man pinch the thighs of his khakis and tug them up so that he could squat comfortably on his haunches to study Willie, who found himself staring into the man's crotch, a place he did not wish to contemplate. "That would have been the end of you, my friend. Clara she has a tremendous kick. She is a fine soccer player. She can put it in the goal from the centre line." Breathing loudly through his nose and moustache, the man now said, "I estimate the crop is worth sixty-five or even seventy thousand dollars. Correct?" He tipped his head to one side to regard Willie more clearly in the half-light of the hallway. His head was a perfect dome, skull plates fitted under a tarp of scalp. Somewhere, in the world outside, in that blue-skied July afternoon where decent people lived decent lives — where kids flew kites, where mothers made Kool-Aid and dads washed cars — he heard a dog bark. "Am I close? Seventy thousand dollars?"

Willie lay on his side, one hand under his face cushioning his cheek as if he were trying to sleep; it was the hand with which he'd torn away the car deodorizer and it smelled of Attar of Rose, the scent raising a range of regrets that travelled across his mind, chief among them the wish that he'd stayed in the construction business. The bald man now shifted closer, bringing with him his body odour, a stink as searing as ammonia, Attar of Armpit, and held his forefinger in front of Willie's face, held it there as though an object of interest, an artefact found in a Turkish antique shop or Egyptian bazaar. Then he demonstrated how the finger could bend. "Amazing, yes? I mean, when you think of it, it is amazing. You say to it: bend, and it bends."

He then proceeded to drive that forefinger into Willie's

right ear — drive it hard forcing Willie's head against the wall. The forefinger felt like a hammer handle and Willie tried to move away but the finger drove deeper, until he began fearing for the very bones of his skull and his brain within. He managed to cry out causing the other two to caw with laughter. When the bald man withdrew his finger he wiped it on Willie's shoulder, back and forth like a bloody blade. "So what's it going to be, my friend?" Before Willie could respond the bald man added, "I can stick it a few other places. I can do that. Or I could give you nose job. You would like nose job?" He glanced up at his henchmen, one black eyebrow cocked questioningly. "Nose job?"

"Yeah, yeah, give him a nose job," said Myron.

"Clara?"

The woman shook her hair away from her face and shrugged as if she were bored with nose jobs.

The bald man pinched Willie's nose high up at the bridge and squeezed just enough to give a taste of the power in his grip. Willie bayed like a scalded hound and the bald man tilted his ear toward Willie preparing to be a good listener.

Willie told all. He described everything, the hike through the bush, the narcs, the ditch, the orchard, the old beehives; he even offered to draw a map.

Still squatting on his haunches, the bald man considered this narrative. The level of detail was impressive enough to be convincing, and his air of innocent contemplation almost made him seem a reasonable chap, someone who had happened along and found poor Willie and listened to his tale of woe. The bald man pursed his lips and contracted his brow and nodded his head. "I would say," he began, "that we are going for drive."

⁌

The bald man's name was Steve, and they had shrewdly parked the van two streets over near a mini-mall. Just as they were about to get into the van, Steve's cell rang. He tweezed it up from the front pocket of his black jeans, flipped it open and cleared his throat. "Yes," he said in the calm and stentorian tone of a man in absolute command, though within seconds he began to retreat, tried to get a word in but couldn't, so nodded, blew a big puff of air, put his palm to his head, gestured as if to make a point, but, his gesture wilting, his arm falling, shut his eyes and gave in to defeat. When he at last got a chance to speak it was in some language Willie could only judge as vaguely Slavic. Steve finally slapped the cell shut and without looking at Myron or Clara, said, "Wait." He strode from the van into the convenience store in the mini-mall and emerged a few minutes later carrying a bag of groceries, the glare in his eyes daring any of them to smirk.

He and Willie sat on the rear bench, Steve with his arm stretched out along the top of the seatback and around Willie's shoulders, as if they were the sort of old-time buddies unthreatened by a little physical contact, and earthy enough to be unconcerned by the smell of an unvarnished man. Myron drove and Clara sat up front with him strumming "Truckin'" on the bat. The grocery bag sat on the floor between Steve and Willie's feet, and Willie could see it contained cat food, tampons, a ten-pack of Mars Bars, and diapers. A father? Was it possible that Steve was a dad, that he had a child, that later today, tonight, he'd return to some house where a woman waited with their baby, a baby he'd take in his arms and hold, kiss, croon over, or, if it was asleep, gaze lovingly upon?

It was only a few blocks to the nearest bank and Willie had the painful opportunity to observe the lives of other people, people who, for all the routine and drudgery of their wage-slave lives, were not on this Saturday afternoon being beaten and robbed and kidnapped.

"Myron, stay. Clara, come."

Clara hopped out of the front and opened the van's sliding door. Before they got out, Steve gripped Willie by the back of the neck and gave a brief squeeze, a squeeze fierce enough to make Willie flinch, enough to remind him of the awful crushing power that lay in wait for those who misbehaved. He also held his hammer-handle forefinger in front of Willie's nose as a reminder of the places it could go and the damage it could do.

"You understand, farm boy?"

"Yes."

"Good. Very good." Steve clapped him not unamiably on the chest. Steve's forearms were forested in black hair that partially obscured the Oriental dragons tattooed on them — the scaly tails executed with considerable artistry in gold and green and blue. He nudged Willie, who got out and stood on the strip of grass that ran between the curb and the sidewalk beside a large old maple. In the seconds during which he waited obediently for Steve, Willie lamented not having paid enough attention to grass and maple trees during his life, a lapse that he would correct if he survived. Steve stepped out and, confident that Willie wasn't going anywhere, turned his broad back to him and gauged the situation. He had a Charles Bronson body, wide-shouldered and narrow hipped, with big hands and square wrists. A boxer, a coal miner, and Willie had no doubt an ex-con, a man familiar with the courtroom, a man able to distinguish the rich *chuk* of the locks on a lawyer's tooled leather briefcase snapping shut from the clang of a jail cell, a man who knew the world of the institution, the odour of a cell, the corridors of power and powerlessness. Steve now faced Willie and extended his arm usherlike, inviting him — if it was not too much trouble — to cross the road.

Willie began jabbering, "My account's empty man, I'm telling you I got nothing, and the pot deal it's all fucked up, I don't know —"

Steve put his arm around Willie in a brotherly hug and whispered, "Shush," and in this way they rounded the corner to the bank with Clara crooning "Money," by Pink Floyd.

That was how Lance and Rex and Darrel, emerging from McDonald's two doors down eating ice-cream cones, saw them.

For an instant, Willie's gaze locked with Lance's as Clara held the door and Steve guided Willie on in. That instant was long enough for Willie to see Lance concluding, through his one functioning eye, that his suspicions were correct and that Willie had indeed fucked them royally; fucked them, betrayed them, screwed them over, stabbed them in the back and up the ass. Steve and Clara had not noticed the three men they'd so brutally assaulted scarcely twenty-four hours ago. Maybe it was the fact that Lance, Rex, and Darrel were eating ice-cream cones, or that Steve and Clara were too intent on the task at hand. Inside the bank, an elderly security guard chatted with a woman in the lineup to the teller; the machines were free, and Steve herded Willie straight to the nearest one and handed him his wallet. It took Willie three tries to get his ATM card into the slot.

Steve rested his plank-thick palm on the metal ledge and counselled him, "Big breath, Willie, big breath, yes, good, very good."

Willie almost felt grateful. He took that breath and then another, suppressed a sob, and then keyed in the numbers of his code and tried to withdraw the maximum, four hundred dollars, but after interminable seconds during which the display window cheerfully encouraged him to invest in home-owner's insurance, he was informed that his account contained insufficient funds. He tried three hundred, then two hundred, then one hundred, and was finally permitted to withdraw forty. Holding the two twenty-dollar bills, he turned to Steve, who chewed his lower lip and then asked what other accounts he had?

"This is it." Willie flinched, fearing the dagger-thrust of Steve's forefinger.

Steve slowly shook his head as if this presented him no alternative but to do what he had to do — what any reasonable man would do in these circumstances.

"I'm telling you —" began Willie, seeking a sincerity of pitch that would convince anyone, Satan himself, that he spoke the truth. He glanced toward Clara, hoping that a female, gentler, kinder, more understanding, would believe him; she flexed her fist around the bat.

Steve placed his slab of a hand on Willie's shoulder and

turned him toward the door which Clara opened. With Steve leading and Clara in the rear, they escorted Willie back around the corner and across the street toward Myron who was waiting in the van.

"Looks like he's got a stick up his ass," sneered Clara, who clearly did not much like young Myron, and seemed to be competing with him for Steve's approval.

Myron did indeed appear to have adopted an awkwardly erect pose. Steve, shrewd, experienced, wise in the ways of the underworld, read the panic in Myron's eyes. Casually raising his hand as if to stroke his moustache and shield his mouth, he hissed to Clara, "Go around the front." He then changed courses toward the van's rear. At that moment Willie realized he'd been forgotten, and in seconds Clara and Steve were two full car lengths ahead of him; it was also at that moment that Steve looked back. For an instant the look they shared was like that shared by Willie and Lance just moments before, a look brief but weighty, a look laden with meaning, a look containing perhaps even a measure of sorrow: *Don't run*, said the look, *don't betray me, not now, for we've gone so far together. Besides, I could hurt you, indeed I will hurt you, I will make you bleed, for you are the rabbit and I am the wolf, and therein lies a relationship that is as unalterable as it is ancient....*

Adrenalin blunting the pain in his ankle, Willie ran like a hare.

CHAPTER 12

THE WASHROOM OF Dunkin' Donuts had fluorescent track lighting, one tube of which was shorted out and twitching, the wires dangling like frayed nerves. A previous patron had unspooled a roll of toilet paper, garlanding the stalls in a festive manner while someone else had drawn a gibbet on the mirror in red crayon and a stick man dangling with a broken neck. This was quite likely the longest day Willie had ever known, certainly the longest since the day Mercedes left him for the last time and he knew, finally, that it was finished. That day and this were not so different, for he knew that his pot-growing days were also finished; this was not the life for him.

He regarded himself in the mirror. Steve's abuse had crammed yet more injuries into his already overcrowded body:

a bruised cheek, a cut lip, an ear plugged with clotted blood, a ribcage that felt as if it had been used as an anvil. The worst of it though was unseen: his wrists, his elbows, his shoulders and of course his sprained ankle were all groaning in their sockets while his lungs ached at each breath as if stitched with fish hooks. He'd escaped Steve by limping up Main, had got himself caught in the doors of a bus as it was pulling away, clung to the pole for the next three stops while searching his pockets for the fare — discovering that somehow he'd managed to keep the two twenties he'd withdrawn from the ATM — but found all his change except one single penny had gone to phone calls that morning. He'd edged his way down to the rear doors and jumped off at the fourth stop and run through a Laundromat into an alley where he lay under a car with an oil leak. He would have stayed there on the warm tarmac but a woman emerged lugging a canvas sack of clothes and got into the vehicle, started it, slammed it in drive and was rolling almost before Willie could wriggle his way out. He went back through the Laundromat, oil stain seeping bloodlike down his back, plucked a newspaper from the recycling box and pretended to read. After a few seconds he threw it down and hobbled his way to the donut shop toilet. He envisioned Clara and Darrel squaring off with their baseball bats, but doubted that Lance and Company were any match for Steve and crew.

Emerging from the washroom, Willie bought a powdered donut and a cup of coffee and then dropped into a booth and sat there slumped and stunned.

When Carmen saw him her face crumpled. She reached out then recoiled as if the slightest touch might complicate his condition.

As drubbed and numb as he was, he could still view the scene from afar. *Yes, Carmen, see how I suffer. Behold the agonies I endure for us, for you. . . .*

Carmen was wearing black jeans, a crimson T-shirt, and a grey cardigan, her fists curled inside the sleeves. Putting her hand in her mouth her eyes grew wide as she sucked the cardigan's cuff and began to weep. Her forehead looked more bulbous than ever, lending a childlike quality to her teary face.

Willie reached out and drew her down next to him while Rollo seated himself on the opposite bench. Carmen pulled her hand from her mouth, draped her arms around Willie and continued to cry, her soft warm body convulsing not unappealingly against him while he noted that she smelled strongly of unfamiliar soap. Did Rollo, he wondered, smell the same?

"The fuck happened?" hissed Rollo keeping his head low to the table.

As Willie explained, Carmen listened, and soon stopped sobbing and leaned further and further away the more she heard, the back of her wrist across her mouth, her eyes growing wide with horror as if besieged by ghouls. Yet fear was suddenly replaced by indignation and she balled her fist and slugged Willie on the shoulder. "I told you," she said through clenched teeth. "I told you they were out there."

"That was my parents' house," moaned Rollo. "I grew up in that house."

Willie was less concerned about Rollo's heritage than about

a change in Rollo's face. Something was different.

"Now can we please go to Mexico? Huh?" She tried to glare but her face collapsed and she wept again. "Oh God, I'm sorry, Willie. Look at what they did to you."

By now the other patrons — skateboarders, a mother and three kids, a couple of salesmen, a vagrant with a shopping cart parked outside the door heaped with bottles and cans — were all watching.

"I want a cigarette," stated Carmen, petulant, defiant. She wiped her eyes and scanned for a fellow addict. "I need a cigarette. Does anyone have a cigarette?" she called, as if pleading for a doctor. The faces looked at her blankly. Then the bum came shuffling over in his overcoat and baseball cap and tipped a soup tin full of butts toward her as if it was a candy jar. "That's very kind of you, sir." She sorted through and selected one and thanked him again, and he shuffled off.

"Carmen that's disgusting," said Willie.

"I didn't want to insult him." She smiled and held the butt up and nodded again as the bum, outside the window now, leaned his weight into his shopping cart and headed off.

Willie felt strangely calm. With pain raging like a caged ape throughout his body and thugs hunting him, a strange serenity welled up within as if an emotional breaker switch had been tripped releasing a dose of endorphins. And with it came clarity and suspicion. He imagined Rollo and Carmen in a hotel room together, in a hotel room shower, soaping each other's naked bodies. He imagined the suds, Carmen's soap-slick thighs, and heard her groans of pleasure. Willie swallowed. It felt as if he had a fist in his throat. He studied Carmen and

Rollo now: Carmen's mascara was running so that she looked like an extra in a horror film, and she was gnawing her knuckle right through that cardigan. He'd always liked that cardigan; it looked comfortable and secure and made him think of kittens curled on a blanket. How could she sleep with Rollo? *Had she slept with Rollo?*

Willie turned to him — and realized what was different about his look: he'd shaved his soul patch. It was gone, replaced by a pale spot beneath his lower lip, all the more noticeable in contrast to his tan. Rollo had been sporting that soul patch for a decade, it was his signature, and yet some time between last night and this afternoon he'd decided to get rid of it. Staring at that raw-looking spot, Willie shook his head clear. "So, Rollo. You call the guy?"

"He didn't answer."

"Call him again."

Carmen gripped Willie's hands and leaned toward him whispering, "Mexico, Willie, Mexico."

He slid his hand from beneath hers and patted it soothingly though kept his gaze upon Rollo. Willie had bought her the cardigan at a Christmas craft market where everyone had been fragrant and calm. It was alpaca. The alpaca, so he had read on the artfully lettered card, was cousin to the llama and native to the Andes. Carmen loved alpaca. She loved alpaca so much she'd taken off her clothes and put on the sweater so as to feel it against her skin; never had she looked lovelier, and rarely had she been so sensual as on that snowy pre-Christmas evening, but the sweater had lost its sensual allure because Carmen now smelled of the same soap as Rollo, salty and sweet and a little acrid. Or was he mistaken? Could he rely on his senses at this moment? Suddenly Willie threw himself across the tabletop and grabbed Rollo by his shirt, but instead of head-butting him, instead of shrieking accusations, instead of biting his throat, he sniffed him, he shoved his nose into Rollo's neck and inhaled.

Rollo flailed and squealed as if a reptile was crawling up out of his shirt.

"Willie!" Carmen grabbed him.

Willie sat back down. Rollo was breathing heavily and staring in horror as if he'd made a pass. Willie looked at Carmen, whose eyes were skating side to side as if seeking a way out of their sockets. He studied those eyes. "You two smell of the same soap," he said.

She said nothing and looked as though she might be sick.

Willie turned to Rollo whose face had taken on a strangely flat look as if enduring a gale-force wind. "Phone him."

Rollo obediently began punching numbers on his cell. Willie could see through his fine blond hair to his pale raw skull. The human skull was only the thickness of a penny. His dad had owned a pair of penny loafers with shiny new pennies in the slots in the leather uppers. He imagined how easily a ballpeen hammer would pop a neat round hole in Rollo's skull, he thought of Clara nearly kicking a hole in his sternum, he thought of Steve nearly driving his forefinger in through Willie's skull and into his brain matter. It would be easy to get the hammer stuck in Rollo's skull. Maybe he'd survive with some curious brain injury that left him fluent in Finnish. Still holding Carmen's hand, Willie's imagination turned to the one thing worse than Rollo making love to Carmen, which was Carmen making love to Rollo, passionate love, ecstatic love, crying out and clutching him. . . . Had Carmen and Rollo betrayed him? Trembling with pain and indignation, Willie suddenly demanded, "Where were you last night, Carmen?"

Her glance cut toward Rollo then back to Willie. Her throat churned as she swallowed. "The Johnny Canuck."

He let the silence spread between them like an expanding blood stain. "What name did you use?"

"Mine. Carmen Conway," she whispered.

How hurt she looked at such suspicion, but it was Willie who suffered. "And you, Rollo?"

"Me what?"

"Where were you?"

"Home, man, home."

Willie stared at each of them in turn, saying nothing, and feeling the grim vigour of his righteous indignation. How easy it would be to pass on the violence that he had received from Steve. His hand trembled with the desire to strike out, to take up the sugar dispenser and bash Rollo's face.

"Willie . . ." Carmen clutched beseechingly at his arm. "I love you."

Maybe she did. Maybe she and Rollo just happened to both use the same soap. Maybe she'd been scared and drunk and Rollo had taken advantage. Or maybe Willie was a putz. One thing was certain: without money he was nothing. He said to Rollo, "Call the guy again. We'll cross the border and meet him in Blaine. We'll get this done."

They watched Rollo resume stabbing at his cellphone and

waited as he listened to it ring and ring. He shrugged. "Nothin'."

"We have to go, now," said Willie.

"Go get your van," said Rollo. "We'll wait here."

Willie stared at Rollo. *We'll* wait here? He glanced at Carmen, who had gone so white she was almost translucent. Veins were pulsing in her temples. She tried to speak but couldn't. Willie said, quietly, reasonably, "Your car's right here, Rollo."

Rollo sat back palms out as if keeping Willie at bay. "No the fuck way. They know my car. They'll be watching."

"And my van's at your place," Willie reminded him. "They're probably tearing it to pieces right now."

Carmen stood and announced the tragic news: "I have to go to the bathroom." She fled.

Willie watched her rush down the corridor between the booths and then he turned back to Rollo. "Juliet."

It took Rollo only an instant. "What? Yeah! Juliet! Brilliant!"

Willie was able to savour a moment of quiet pride at having come up with a solution. Rollo slid his phone across the starred Formica and Willie punched the glowing numbers; Juliet answered on the first ring, she was just stepping out the door to pick up Angela and drive her down to Seattle.

❧

And so once again Willie was slicing along Highway 99 South toward the border. The Caddie was a shark, a beast, its engine eating the road, the air molecules scattering from its path. Willie, Carmen, and Rollo slouched low in the rear seat while

Angela sprawled up front with Juliet. Angela was not at all pleased with this sudden unexpected company and she made her opinion known.

"Great, Dad. Real proud to know you. You look like you just got punched out in a bar."

"Do you have any idea what your father has been through?" demanded Carmen. "Look at him."

Rather than turn around, Angela sank down in either shame or fatigue. She was wearing a red bandana pirate style over her hair and gold hoop earrings. "I saw, Carmen."

"You saw."

She blew up. Kneeling on the seat she thrust her face into Carmen's. "Yes! I saw!" Tears spurted from her eyes. "I saw." She spoke quietly now, sincerely, as if she'd reached the end of her endurance. "I hate you, Carmen. I really, really hate you. I hate your paintings, and I hate your big lumpy forehead —"

"Angela! Stop," pleaded Willie.

As if vindicated by Angela's display, Carmen said nothing, merely looked off out the window while Willie asked Rollo what kind of car Lance drove.

Rollo got defensive. "I don't know, man. A car!"

"There's binoculars in the glove compartment," said Juliet. "You want to keep an eye on the other cars, go for it." Angela handed them back over her shoulder. Eye-level with the window ledge, Willie tried focusing on the other cars but soon began feeling motion-sick. Juliet saw him in the rear-view. "Your face is green, Willie. No hurling on the upholstery."

"Carmen, do you have any more codeine?"

She dug into her front pocket and came up with the brown

plastic bottle and shook it. They all recognized the sad rattle of a single tablet.

"Here." Juliet passed back a fresh bottle.

"Dad, you'll get constipation, not to mention liver damage," said Angela.

Willie popped off the cap, punctured the safety seal, pried out the cotton, swallowed three, washed them down with a gulp of warm Diet Pepsi and held on until the nausea and pain and all the other suspicion and misery passed like a marching band into the distance. Shutting his eyes he let his head loll. All they had to do was contact the broker and point the guy to where the pot was stashed and they were home free. They didn't even have to touch it themselves. He took some relief in the fact that Steve had dismissed the map that Willie had grovellingly offered to draw, opting instead for a personal guide. Still, Steve and Clara and Myron could have already crossed the border and be driving around looking for an old orchard with a beehive. It wouldn't be visible from the road so they'd have a lot of footwork and trespassing to do, and might just give up and go home, or bring the police down on themselves. Or maybe they'd lurk near the border knowing Willie would cross sooner or later and then follow him. He envisioned the ultimate humiliation of being beaten to a whimpering lump in front of his ex-mother-in-law, daughter and girlfriend. A bout of cramps seized his gut making him groan.

"Dad?"

"Willie?"

He clenched his teeth and shook his head.

"We're almost at the border," said Juliet. "Your shirt, Willie.

The blood? Nice touch. The guards'll love it. And the split lip and all the other stuff. They'll never notice." She put the blinker on and took the exit toward White Rock. "We're going shirt shopping," she said. "And then we're going to take the powder puff to you. And then," she added, finally, "we're going to make a phone call." They slowed as they drove along a gently curving two-lane walled in by tall dark fir trees, the forest opening here and there to reveal horses in fields, farmhouses, and, as they neared White Rock, gated communities of mauve and taupe condominiums. Eventually they came in view of the ocean, and descended to the beachfront where Juliet drove slowly past the pier and the enormous whitewashed rock for which the town was named. They parked overlooking railroad tracks and the sea. Juliet stepped on the pedal engaging the emergency brake then turned and rested her elbow on the seatback. "These other guys," she said. "The poachers. The ones who know where it is. What're they driving?"

Willie described the Econoline van, circus-strongman Steve, baseball-bat Clara, and young Myron.

"Guys. It's called the border patrol," said Angela. "There's a hotline."

Juliet considered this and then batted her eyelashes at Willie. "She ain't as dumb as she looks."

"But what if they've done it to us, too?" cut in Carmen.

"The car's clean. We're clean." Juliet stared at each of them in turn, ending with Angela. "Aren't we?"

Angela sat lower in her seat, crossed her arms tightly, set her jaw and avoided her grandmother's gaze.

Juliet's voice got big with impatience, a voice Willie recognized from the days when she used to babysit her wilful granddaughter. "*An*gela," she said, emphasizing the first syllable, "we're clean, aren't we?"

"Fuck." Angela hauled a bag of pot from her purse.

"See that," said Carmen. "She stole from you, Willie. She steals from her father."

Juliet did not deign to involve herself in any of this. She got out then looked back into the car before closing the door. "Fifteen minutes."

Angela swung her door wide whacking the car next to them. "Well, don't leave me with *them*."

Carmen, meanwhile, was listing her lost assets. "I've lost my art books, my paintings, my clothes, my house, my home, everything!" Willie's failure to react with due remorse enraged Carmen, who decided to punish him by ruining her health. "I need a smoke." She climbed over Rollo and got out of the car and headed off in the direction Juliet and Angela had gone.

Willie and Rollo exhaled together and said nothing, the only sounds the sighing and settling of the Caddie's motor, the cars cruising past behind them, and the muted music from the radios down on the beach. There was the smell of oily gravel and creosote from the tracks and the salty scent of the sea where sailboats stood like peaked napkins on a blue table.

"You slept with Carmen," said Willie.

Rollo reacted like Willie had spat in his face. "Aw, man! Come on. Me?"

Willie contemplated strangling Rollo and shoving him into the trunk. The caddie had a trunk big enough to take half a dozen Rollo's. They could just make a little detour before the border and deposit him in a ditch. Carmen's reaction would tell him a lot; if she was relieved it would be a good sign. "I made a few phone calls last night."

"I dropped her off, Willie, I dropped her off."

Rollo was sweating. Rollo rarely sweated, but there it was, little droplets beading his forehead and in the pale bare spot where his soul patch used to live. Where was the cool of the Chicago Jazz Man now? Was it fear or the strain that came with insisting upon his innocence? Willie gazed off out the window and said, "That's where I'd like to be. Out on a boat."

"Man when this is done you can buy yourself a boat," said Rollo eagerly encouraging his good buddy Willie to pursue such idyllic fantasies. "I'll help you."

Willie was savouring Rollo's anguish. Willie shut his eyes and angled his face to the sun shining in through the car window and basked. He was five years old and they were at the beach and he was happy. His dapper dad was in a jolly mood, a gold chain glinting around his neck and a gold watch on his wrist; his mother was smiling in her frosted lipstick, straw sun hat and yellow polka-dot bikini; everything smelled of Coppertone and all was well. There was an inner tube tied to the roof of the Chev and they were going to paddle out on the glittering sea.

But he was not five years old. He was in trouble and the man next to him may well have seduced his woman; worse, his woman may have gone along with it. At that moment all he wanted was for the issue to be settled, to know the truth one way or the other even if the news was bad. Maybe it would be better if they had betrayed him, for then at least he'd be able to move on.

Reaching into the front seat for Angela's bag of pot, he saw a magazine on the seat open to an ad for the Athena spa in Santa Barbara: a sunrise on the beach featuring a couple with their arms raised as if in worship. That was all, the sunrise, the sea, the sand, two people born anew, and at the bottom a phone number and a website address. Willie scarcely paused as he grabbed the baggie of dope, but his glance took it all in: an image of optimism and hope though with a hint of the cult about it.

He began extricating himself from the car.

"Man," grovelled Rollo, eager to help his best buddy Willie. "Hold on. Lemme help you."

Willie sat suddenly still and addressed Rollo without looking at him. "Rollo. Stay." It was an eerie realization that Willie had used Steve's voice and phrasing, even a hint of his accent. Upright at last, he limped across the parking lot to a yellow-domed garbage bin and punched the bag of pot through the flap. He looked back toward the car where Rollo sat low in the seat. Maybe Carmen *had* been at the Johnny Canuck last night under her own name and he, exhausted and confused, had been talking to an equally exhausted and confused hotel desk clerk who'd mistaken or misheard the name? Or maybe he'd called the wrong Johnny Canuck? How many Johnny Canucks were there? Fatigue and pharmaceuticals awarded him the rare faculty of simplifying his mind and emotions, and he decided not to think about it. He wandered over to the railroad tracks and looked out over the ocean. The sun soothed his head and neck and back. Oh, to lie down in the hot sand and sleep. . . . He hadn't slept in thirty hours. His shadow lay across the tracks. When they went to the beach it had been a tradition that his dad would give him a penny to place on the track, then they'd watch the train — Great Northern Railway, a mountain goat painted on each of the vast iron cars — flatten the coin, crush the queen's head with its necklace and hairdo and crown right out of existence, leaving that copper disc so hot he'd juggle it in his hands and his dad would laugh and put his arm around his shoulders, and the world was good. Willie found a coin in his pocket, a penny; he tried to place it on the rail but was too stiff to bend. He lowered himself to one knee and, like an arthritic worshipper at an altar, managed to place the coin.

*

"Willie." Juliet was standing by the driver's door holding up a plastic bag, making it swing side to side as if to lure him back, as if he were an old dog that had been let out to pee and had forgotten where it lived. He looked once more at the serene sea and then at the penny on the track, and returned to the car, which is when they all realized that Carmen was missing. Willie grew convinced that this was a trial of the sort found in mythology: he must pass three terrors and cross three bridges before finding his prize, but the terrors would spawn other terrors, and the bridges mirror themselves in the water they spanned, creating infinities of rivers and bridges to be crossed, so his trials would become an eternal quest — no, a curse. He went off in search of Carmen.

White Rock was in full swing; the taut and tanned mingled with the pale and flabby in the ice cream parlours, coffee boutiques and trinket stalls. They shuffled along the sidewalk past overflowing trash bins and parked cars that glinted so sharply Willie had to avert his eyes. In the street, the cars rolling by added their exhaust to the parched air, an ongoing smear of rap and reggae, suburban white boys getting down and looking mean. A bum browsing the bins with a wicker basket over his forearm picked through the refuse with a pair of lacquered black chopsticks. Willie admired the man's utter indifference to the contempt of passersby. Eventually Willie spotted Carmen in a small gallery standing before a print of one of Frida Kahlo's self-portraits: her eyes glowing braziers beneath those famous brows that met in a dark ridge, pride and pain crashing together like seas. Willie watched Carmen for a while, her face softened by awe and haloed by a soft radiance that came from attending so rapturously, so respectfully, to something other than herself.

He spoke quietly. "Carmen."

After a moment she turned and wiped her eyes and smiled, the way she used to when she woke in the morning and saw him, a first reaction, sincere and spontaneous. She held out her hand to him and they returned to the car where Juliet proceeded to mask his scrapes with her makeup brushes.

CHAPTER 13

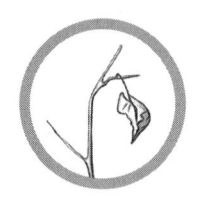

SHE PEELED UP THE FLOOR MATS, emptied the ashtray and the glovebox, aimed a flashlight up under the seats, hauled the spare tire from the trunk, then lifted the hood and leaned like a mechanic to study the motor, all the while maintaining an amiable banter as if they were friends at an antique car show and she was not, in fact, trying to find dope or anthrax or the makings of a bomb and jail them for the rest of their lives.

"It's balmy, isn't it? Isn't it balmy weather we're having?"

"Balmy," agreed Juliet.

"It was a wet spring," the officer said, angling a mirror on a pole to see up under the chassis. She wore a uniform and a gun and a name tag that said C. Spencer. Her greying hair was cut close to the skull and her earlobes resembled that part on a plucked chicken called the pope's nose. She looked about forty and her belt cut a deep crease in her belly. "But it's been a balmy summer." Willie kept looking at the vehicles proceeding through customs, fearing he'd spot the van with Steve and Clara and Myron. Juliet had assured him she'd got through to U.S. Customs and given a thorough description, but what if the message got lost, what if they'd already gone through, or had switched vehicles?

Agent Spencer kicked at the tires then lowered herself to one knee and with a screwdriver pried off the hubcap, and squinted into it. She went around the car going through the same slow procedure with all the hubcaps. Finding nothing, she pushed herself upright and slapped the grit from her palms. She wore a wristwatch complex with dials and digits and buttons. "Well." C. Spencer stood back from the car as if about to make an offer on it. She lifted and resettled her hat further back on her head, bunched her lips then twisted them to one side and sniffed. For a moment Willie almost expected her to ask them for suggestions as to what she might tear apart next. "I guess that's about it for you folks. Have a good one."

⁂

They passed the Denny's Willie had sat in, sped by the Pastime Tavern and the Seaview porn theatre, and the lines of Canadian cars waiting to buy cheap gas at an Arco station. Off to the right the sea gleamed like oil and there came the stink of mud and clams.

"Turn up here," said Willie. He and Carmen were side by

side in the back, thighs touching, still basking in the warmth of reconciliation.

They left the trailer courts of Blaine, where even the sorriest white trash proudly displayed the stars and stripes, for they were not just any old trailer trash, they were American trailer trash, which is to say God's trailer trash, and it was their birthright to partake of that self-imposed glory. The Caddie drove by pastures, overgrown barns and the occasional stand of fruit trees. Everything looked different in the daylight, and it took a few turns for Willie to orient himself. "Here. No. Wait. Keep going."

"Take your time, baby," said Carmen, giving his hand a reassuring squeeze.

Willie was grateful for this indulgence even as he sensed she was beginning to overdo it. Her sudden demonstrativeness was a touch embarrassing in front of Juliet and Angela. He was about to start explaining again how dark and disorienting it had been, but then he spotted the trailer court. "Here! Just up here." He directed Juliet to the place where he had waded through the blackberry bushes and climbed over the wire fence. Juliet pulled over as far as she could and turned off the ignition, and in the silence they all glanced around. Nothing. The road was empty. Then everyone was looking at Willie. Herein lay the satisfaction of being the central figure. Five people with him in the middle — the hub.

He got out of the car and discovered that the grass was still trampled from the path he'd made last night. He followed it through and reached the barbed wire and there, not thirty feet away, stood the hives. He listened then climbed through and ran at a crouch to the stacked crates. Again he glanced around. In the daylight he could see that many of the trees were cobwebbed with tent caterpillars. Maybe a hundred yards off was the house, dating to the early years of the century by the looks of it. He lifted the first box — empty. He lifted the second — empty. He dropped to his knees and searched. He looked for another set of boxes, no, there were no others. Gone. It was gone. They'd beat him to it. That's why the grass was so flattened. He pitched forward with his head in his hands and face in the dirt, and cried out again letting the earth absorb his anguish. He stayed there, rocking forward and back like a devotee pleading mercy from some arcane god.

"Dad?"

Willie got to his feet and wiped the soil from his face. Angela didn't need much more explanation. He had not stood so broken before his daughter since Mercedes left, and he could see that she didn't like it now any more than she had then.

"You're such a fucking asshole, Dad." Then she hugged him. "And you've gone and ruined your makeup," she added.

Desperate to regain even a dime of dignity, Willie tried to laugh but winced at his split lip. He managed a small smile as if he were already well past the stages of rage and denial and moving on to the next phase, acceptance. And even as deep inside himself he keened like a soul condemned, he took an airy interest in the orchard with its blighted fruit trees and remarked in a cheerful voice, "Well, this place has seen better days."

Angela nodded. They had their arms around each other's waists. Willie felt her gauging him, wondering what he would do, how he would react, and no doubt hoping he'd keep it together and not get all embarrassing on her or go to pieces. He tried to think that losing the dope was a small price for such a moment with his daughter, but he didn't believe it; he wanted both, his daughter and his dope. His heart felt like a brick. They heard rustling and saw Rollo then Carmen and finally Juliet appear at the fence. Rollo looked hopeful, Carmen looked questioning, Juliet knew it was gone. Then they all knew. And then the three of them saw something else. Willie and Angela turned and saw a woman approaching, a tall woman in her forties, with long thick auburn hair, jeans and a T-shirt with the Apple computer logo on one breast. With her was Ed.

Ed didn't seem in the slightest bit surprised, he merely turned to the woman. "That's him. That's the guy."

Willie's eyes widened as though he'd been picked from a police lineup.

The woman faced Willie with new interest. "Him?"

Ed nodded. "Yup."

"Lies, all lies," said Willie, choking out a laugh.

"You mean you're not a great guy?"

"Well, that part's true."

"Just not a good navigator," she said. "Driveway's on the other side." She glanced at Ed, who merely shrugged at the eccentricities of good-neighbour Willie and pulled out his smokes. "Or were you just hunting for honey?" she asked, noting the scattered hive crates. She was smiling, but there was more than amused curiosity in her tone. Willie looked to the others who were still on the far side of the barbed wire fence and were leaving the explanations up to him.

He introduced Angela and said they were driving her down

to Seattle because she was going to school there. "And we decided to take the scenic route. And I remembered Ed saying how he'd probably be down here too."

"Diane." As she extended her hand a brass bracelet in the form of a snake swallowing its tail slid down her wrist. She had a firm grip and considered Willie with appraising eyes. Some of her Lady Godiva hair had spilled over her shoulders. There was plenty to go around, and it was not only auburn but streaked with the warm tones of sandstone.

"Jesus John Christ," said Ed, getting a closer look at Willie's face. "The hell's all over your face?"

Willie's hand went up to his cheek and he felt the dirt and sweat and the powder. "Slipped on the stairs."

Ed frowned and pulled his head back and regarded Willie as though he was not buying it. Ed was tactful enough, however, not to pursue it, rather to consign it to the confused world of minds other than his own. "Come on in for a cider."

"Oh, gee, no, really, we have to get going."

But Ed was having none of that. "'How many pleasures have been enjoyed by robbers, patricides, tyrants.'"

Diane looked at Willie and rolled her eyes as if asking whether he always did this. "What the hell does that mean?"

"Means it's time for a drink." He waved his arm for everyone to follow and turned and started hiking off toward the house.

Rollo and Willie held the strands of barbed wire apart so that Juliet and Carmen could climb through, and they all followed Ed, who was wearing an engineer's cap and oil-stained overalls.

The house was what Willie called Vicwardian, a combination of Victorian and Edwardian, with a few features of Early American farmhouse thrown in. It had a steeply pitched roof with ornate fascias, shiplap siding, some stained glass, and a wraparound porch that was glassed-in at the back.

⁓

They sat in a living room that smelled of warm stone and warm wood, sipping mugs of cider, the mugs ranging from handmade clay to pewter tankards. There were four large leather chairs, two old tuck-and-groove couches with scrollwork arms, and a pair of bentwood rockers. Willie settled himself on a couch next to Carmen with his ceramic mug of sharp-scented cider. The solemn ticking of a grandfather clock was complemented by the afternoon sun highlighting the grain of the fir floor while the apples in the Kashmiri carpet gleamed like a page in an illuminated manuscript. Diane had been a sales rep for Apple computers. She'd quit five years ago to nurse her husband through leukemia, and for the past four had been here alone, trying and failing to make a go of the orchard. She sat in the other rocker with her ankles crossed on a paisley-covered ottoman, wiggling her bare toes.

Nymphs and satyrs flitted in and out of arbours in the faded wallpaper while fat flies lolled on the window ledge. A framed painting of horses running away over the hills hung above the river rock fireplace. On the mantel stood silver candlesticks, and the clock ticked with the resonant rap of a rod on a keg.

Willie wanted to get drunk. He downed his cider fast and, as though understanding his desire, Diane promptly refilled him. Out of habit, he evaluated the house from a builder's point of view, and put it at pre–World War One. As with all houses from that era it combined the seemingly contradictory characteristics of high ceilings and low doorknobs; people being shorter then but somehow requiring more head room. The heat rose in the summer, which was good, but it also rose in the winter, which was bad. The floors were four-inch tongue-and-groove fir slats, and Willie's knees ached in commiseration with the carpenters who had crawled over every foot of the place nailing each slat at twenty-four inch intervals. No pneumatic nail guns or staplers here, just arthritic joints and a mouthful of flooring nails. The ceiling was ribbed with six-by-ten fir beams spaced with lath and plaster, and the corners were raw posts the girth of telephone poles. The timber likely came from the land the house stood on, felled and milled on site by men with axes and whipsaws. The panes in the living room window were slightly rippled meaning they were original. Willie imagined the glaziers scoring and gluing and inhaling glass dust. Labour and craft and more labour. But the place had lasted, and with basic upkeep it would carry on, surviving earthquakes and wind and snow, its only real enemy fire. He wondered if the contractor had left his mark somewhere, carved his initials in some obscure corner like the masons of old. The house's charm only made him feel worse and he stared down into the well of his empty glass.

"Another refill there, Willie?" asked Diane.

He held the glass out and drank deep.

"I like your shirt," Diane said.

He gazed at her through the gold-dust light filling the room. Shirt? Oh, yes, his shirt. He'd hardly noticed it himself. "Juliet got it for me."

Diane smiled at Juliet. "You've got good taste."

The ability to gracefully accept praise was a skill Juliet had mastered and she was also happy to return a compliment. "I love this room," she said, inhaling deeply and looking around to take it all in, to absorb it with all her senses. She had her legs tucked up under her on the old couch and looked regal.

Even Angela had mellowed. "It's like they had pioneer feng shui," she said, basking in the warm glow of late afternoon. "I mean, the way the light comes in. And that glassed-in porch, I love it."

But Willie couldn't bear it: his world was in pieces and here he was required to make polite conversation. "Well," he said. "We should get out of your hair."

Ed protested.

Diane suggested they take a stroll through the orchard because it was too beautiful an afternoon to sit inside.

"No, no," said Willie.

"Yes, yes," said Juliet, mocking him. "Why not?"

Engineer's cap at a jaunty angle, Ed offered his elbow to Juliet who, unable to keep from laughing, was also unable to refuse. They were all on the edge of drunkenness as they travelled out across the grass toward the trees. Willie tried to be brave by taking an interest in their ravaged state.

"Can they be saved?"

"Be expensive," said Diane. "Tent caterpillar, coddling

moth, you name it, they've got it. Things wither when you neglect them." She'd pulled on a long-sleeved checked work shirt and tied her hair in a long loose braid.

Willie regarded the swallows skimming low over the grass. "The birds don't seem to mind."

"Except there's more birds than fruit. And what fruit there is has scab."

They passed a jumble of crates and a broken ladder where Carmen tripped and fell against Willie's back, tearing his new shirt wide open as she clawed for support. The jagged noise of ripping cloth made everyone look. Willie turned to catch Carmen and stood there supporting her by her elbows while she, on her knees, stared up at him, the expression in her eyes wavering between tears and rage. "I want to go home," she whispered.

So did he. "Well, we really do have to get going," he said to the others.

Ed was aghast. "Now? Booze in you? Hell." He frowned and cocked his head to one side as if Willie had said something mildly obscene. "State troopers catch you weaving around the road they'll impound the car and lock you up."

"Juliet's driving."

"I won't allow it," declared Ed, renewing his hold on her arm.

"Scads of room here," said Diane. "Spend the night if you like."

CHAPTER 14

WILLIE WOKE IN THE MIDDLE of the night with a throbbing head and a dry throat, his muscles so stiff he felt encased in plaster. Carmen slept solidly, her back to him, as far away from him as she could get. Groaning through his clenched molars, he managed to roll onto his side and lower himself to the floor, where he remained on all fours until the pain subsided to a manageable agony, then levered himself upright and leaned on the bed, panting, his arms trembling as if in the throes of some palsy. After another minute of deep breathing he embarked upon the journey to the door, found the bathroom down the hall and turned on the light and leaned on the sink. He opened the medicine cabinet and fumbled through the bottles, managing to topple two that went clattering into the sink before he found some aspirin. He swallowed the tablets then drank straight from the faucet and washed his face. When he looked up he found a face in the mirror that might have been pulled from a grave so pale and wretched did it gaze out at him; he shut off the light and stepped back out into the hall. Air, he needed air. Passing the living room he heard Rollo lurch upright.

"It's me."

"Fuckin' Lance's gonna be watching both my places." Rollo's silhouette leaned forward and he put his head in his hands; a sculpture titled *Despair*. How vulnerable he looked, a little boy in his bed.

Willie took some satisfaction in the fact that Rollo's life was poisoned as well as his own, and he wondered if he should put his hand on Rollo's shoulder, maybe pat it, say something like, *there, there.* . . . "You okay?"

"That clock. It's like a coffin."

Willie saw that the grandfather clock did indeed resemble a coffin with a glass lid while the ticking marked the dwindling beats of their lives.

"There's these corpses in Mexico City," said Rollo. "*Las Mommias*, they call 'em. Mummies. A whole underground room in this monastery. Mummified by the chemicals in the soil. They just dry out. They got them displayed in glass-faced coffins. Writhing, man. It's like they woke up in their coffins and flipped out, clawing the walls, shrieking." Rollo raised his hands as if undergoing the very same horror. He swallowed loudly, his voice choked and fearful. "The weirdest thing was their clothes. Their clothes were rags — except for their socks, their socks were perfect."

Willie had never seen Rollo so lost. He found himself taking an almost scientific interest in observing it. "Rollo," he said.

"What?"

"Did you sleep with Carmen?"

The question was delivered so quietly and so suddenly that Rollo could only clutch his blanket to his chest like a startled virgin. "No."

"No?"

"No, man, no."

They remained in the dark with the clock ticking judgelike and disapproving. When it was clear that Rollo had no more to say, Willie went out.

∽

Wearing nothing but his underpants, he stood in the yard and looked at the starlit sky and saw meteors. Of course. The Perseid meteor showers. A mosquito sang in his ear. He swiped at it and flinched at a blade of pain in his shoulder. He wandered across the grass toward the fruit trees. The moon was up and bright enough to cast shadows. The apples might be scabbed and stunted but they smelled sweet. It was almost cool now, and as he walked amid the trees his head began to clear. He kept glancing up and admiring the chalk-dash meteors streaking the night sky. What a busy place it seemed to be up there, while down here the insects chewed and chafed, fell silent as he approached and then resumed once he'd passed.

"What do you think, Willie?"

He staggered.

"Don't have a heart attack. My CPR's rusty." The voice came out of the ground. Diane, stretched out on a blanket. "Are you interested in astronomy? Lie down. It's easier on the neck." Her arm rose, pale in the moonlight, a night-blooming flower unfolding the petals of its fingers to take his hand and lead him down into her subterranean realm. She shifted. "You can share the pillow. Come on."

Embarrassed about being in his undershorts, he nonetheless stretched out and the meteors continued skidding across the sky.

"They used to be called the Tears of Saint Laurence," she said. "As the comet approaches the sun its gases evaporate and the particles are released. That's what we see."

Willie nodded, the pillow soft under his head, the honey smell of Diane's hair mingling with that of the cool night grass, the earth and the apple trees.

"White geese landing on a black celestial sea," she said, as if quoting a line of poetry.

A couple of meteors came skimming in then were gone. "Like flames plunging into water," he said, trying his hand.

"Flaming arrows," said Diane.

"Arrows, yeah." Willie crossed his ankles getting comfortable. It felt good to lie on the earth. He should do it more often, just lie down on his back. "I always wanted an orchard."

She began to laugh quietly.

Willie felt a twinge of embarrassment. "No, really."

"I never wanted an orchard," she said.

"No?"

"Pick fruit, crate fruit, sell fruit, can fruit, juice fruit, cook fruit, eat fruit, drink fruit." She snorted. "Fruit. I'm starting to hate fruit."

"Sell."

"Sell? Well, hell." She began to laugh. "Maybe in a few years. Five. Ten. When the developers get here with the condos. I don't know, I feel kind of committed now. If I ever manage to save the trees you can come back and visit at harvest time and lend a hand. Just don't bring all that pot."

Willie stiffened. His pot? Still here?

"I expected you'd be showing up again. But not that you'd be Ed's neighbour."

"Does Ed know?"

"I don't think so. He knows you're up to something next door, but he's not sure what. Look." The meteors had accelerated. There were schools of them now, like phosphorescent dolphins. The world was upside down and they were in the sky gazing down at the sea. Willie would have been happy to stay that way for the rest of the night, until the stars faded and the sun rose, except for a terrible thought that struck him like a slap in the snoot: Steve. If Diane had found the dope then Steve and his crew were still looking, and might be out there now, at this very moment. And then another thought came to him: maybe she wasn't planning on returning it. Sixty grand would go a long way toward improvements on the farm. It wasn't as if he could do anything about it. Steve, though, would do something about it. Willie sat up.

"What?"

"I have to tell you something."

It didn't take Diane long to grasp the consequences of what

Willie had to say. Bad people were on the hunt, and they were about to arrive, and if they did not find what they were looking for they were going to be angry, and if they were angry they would be violent, and it was Willie who had brought down this plague upon her. Wearing nothing but his undershorts he felt doubly exposed and vulnerable, and so hugged himself as if cold.

Her face was rigid and she spoke in a low voice. "Take your pot and get out of here."

"Diane."

She stood. "Go. Now."

"Diane."

She took her pillow and yanked at her blanket on which he was still sitting. He scrambled to his feet and followed her to the house, feeling not just vulnerable but ridiculous in his undershorts. She showed him his backpack full of pot in a wheelbarrow beneath the lattice-framed porch. By now birds were singing and vermilion light was rising in the eastern sky. He caught her wrist as she was about to head up the back stairs.

"You have to leave, too."

She was amazed. "What?"

"Go to Mexico with Ed. Get out of here for a few days. A week. Until we can be sure they've gone. Until they've given up."

She stared at him as if he was some reptile that had risen up out of the sewer. He took a step back and tried to cover himself, crossing his arms over his chest, apologizing again.

"Just up and leave?"

"You have to. These guys, you don't want to meet them."

"I think I should just call the cops. I don't deserve this," she said.

"No, you don't. Wait. Please. Just wait a minute." He went past her up the steps and inside the house and into the bedroom and, while Carmen slept, silently took his clothes. He dressed in the hallway to the sound of Rollo snoring and the coffin-shaped grandfather clock ticking. When he got back outside Diane, irate and impatient, started in on him again but he interrupted, putting his palms together as if about to pray, and asked her to answer just one question. "What's across the road?"

"What?"

"The other side of the road."

"Nothing. Bush. An empty field."

"That's good. That's great."

She followed Willie back across the orchard to the hives where he picked up the entire stack and headed for the fence. In minutes they'd transferred the boxes to the other side of the road, trampled the grass until it was a virtual highway, then come back across and combed up the grass on this side to cover their passage. The sun was up by the time they got back to the house.

"You should still leave," said Willie.

She looked at him. There were twigs and grass in her endless hair and in her gold cardigan. "This isn't fair."

Willie said nothing, and hoped she didn't cry.

She muttered, "I need a coffee."

It was still dark in the room. Carmen was in bed but not sleeping. "Did you make love to her, Willie?"

"*Carmen....*"

"I got up. I saw you two out there. You were looking at her all evening."

"That's crazy."

"Is it? You know you were walking with a cane when I first met you," she said. She lay with her back to him and spoke to the pine-panelled wall. "Remember? That whole time I was driving I kept thinking: this guy's going to go home and swallow pills. He's going to off himself. I wasn't even supposed to take that call. I scooped you."

"I'm glad you did," said Willie, lying down beside her, getting close, feeling the heat of her body.

He remembered the dark winter afternoon they met. His back was so bad he couldn't drive and had to call a cab. His crew was gone and he'd waited in the carport of that half-finished house that smelled of mud and concrete, watching rain run from the eaves and evaluating the state of his life. Mercedes had left him, Angela blamed him, and his business was in worse condition than his back, on the skids because he refused to build Vancouver Specials. His accountant was warning him of looming disaster, the bank was leaving two and three messages a day, and he hadn't paid his men in a month. When the cab arrived he'd limped out along the two-by-twelve duck-boards. He was wearing a leaky yellow rain slicker, work boots and a hard hat. Carmen had watched in the rear-view mirror as he engineered his way into the back seat and shifted himself about until he found a comparatively pain-free position. He felt as brittle as a piece of old furniture. They talked, two single people on a rainy evening in February, the windshield wipers rhythmic and intimate and the headlights of oncoming cars glaring slickly across the glass. In the front of the cab Carmen had a book on the Mexican muralist Orozco with her. "Look at those colours," she'd kept saying, holding the book open for him at each red light. Later that same evening, in Willie's bed, Carmen told him she wanted to open a laughing club.

"A what?"

"A laughing club. It's a kind of yoga. They have them in Bombay. They get together and everyone laughs. Reduces the stress hormone cortisol and increases endorphins, which relax you."

"Ha ha ha."

"See," she said, "I bet you feel better already."

And he did. They might even have given the laughing club a try if Rollo hadn't so conveniently come through with the seedlings and the house for them to start a grow-op. Moving in with Carmen had involved a triumphant jettisoning of objects reminiscent of Mercedes, as well as a furtive hiding of items too precious to let go, such as his wedding band. He told himself he'd have it melted down and recast for a new ring when he and Carmen got married, but somehow that had yet to happen.

Willie shifted closer to her and put his arm around her. "I've got the pot, Carmen. I've got the pot."

She rolled to face him and studied his eyes. Morning sunlight was expanding the room. Seeing he was telling the truth, she kissed him.

CHAPTER 15

JULIET ACCELERATED THE Caddie onto the I-5 south for Seattle. Angela pried off her Birkenstocks, propped her heels on the dash and paged through a copy of *Rolling Stone*; soon she'd be with Gabriel and away from this crew of goofs. Lulled by the Caddie's hum, the others settled in for the drive. Rollo was happy, plucking an invisible bass, confident about getting hold of Dwayne, the connection, and scoring his commission. Carmen leaned against Willie and dozed off as if slipping into a hot bath. Juliet caught Willie's eye in the rear-view and they exchanged expressions of relief.

"I don't see them anymore," Juliet said.

Ed and Diane had been right behind them for the first mile, but Ed was a cautious driver with a long run ahead of him. Ed was delighted at the unexpected treat of Diane's company while the last look Diane had given Willie had been less than sweet.

They passed Bellingham and in another thirty minutes Everett with its pulp-mill smell of burnt beer sausage. Angela fiddled with the zinc knob of the radio and found a static-free station playing some old Jethro Tull. She was disgusted. "Listen to this, he's singing in praise of a child molester."

"It's a song, Angela," said Juliet.

"'Eyeing little girls with bad intent,'" she quoted. "A song about a filthy old lecher."

"Listen to the flute," said Rollo. "Ripped off Rahsaan Roland Kirk."

For a while Angela and Rollo bonded in their righteous indignation on behalf of Black American musicians robbed by whites. Willie didn't remark that he'd seen Jethro Tull in concert decades ago and rather enjoyed it, and would have been embarrassed to add that Herb Albert and Petula Clark were closer to his heart because he associated them with those happy days before his dad vanished and his mother began drinking.

Eventually they spotted the Seattle Space Needle where the highway began to divide and multiply and Juliet gripped the steering wheel more firmly.

"Next exit," said Angela, navigating. "Then left then right." She was sitting eagerly forward. She cranked the window down. "Feel it? Seattle. The buzz."

Since Rollo's cellphone was out of its range they scanned the street for a booth. Juliet spied one then found a parking place and they waited as Rollo shouldered open the door and hoofed it back to a booth with its glass sides kicked out. Willie drummed his fingers on his knees until, in a gesture of calming reassurance, Carmen gripped them in her own warm hand.

Juliet turned to Angela. "So Gabriel knows how many of us are descending on him?"

"I called him. He's looking forward to meeting you. He's travelled to lots of the places you have, Grandma."

Juliet sounded sceptical. "He has, has he?"

Willie was relieved she was no more approving of this soon-to-be senior citizen diddling Angela than he was. The Seattle air was an asbestos haze as high as they could see and the street-din deafening. The last time Willie had been down here was with Mercedes and Angela, a bitter threesome supposedly on a holiday but in fact in a catfight, claws unfurled, alliances shifting by the minute, the psychological slashing leaving them all lacerated.

The door opened and Rollo lurched in and shook his head.

Willie raked his hand slowly down his face, two days of stubble grating his palm. The smog-muted sun-glare made him squint while the traffic streamed past in a molten flow of plastic and alloy, the people poised in their cars like caught flies in amber. "Great, twenty-five pounds of pot and no buyer."

CHAPTER 16

GABRIEL LIVED IN A CONVERTED WAREHOUSE overlooking Pike Place Market and Elliott Bay. Walking there from the car, they passed a pawnshop with hundreds of pistols in the window. They weren't arranged or sorted or organized, they were simply heaped like old shoes below the counter with little price tags dangling from the trigger guards. Willie, in a dour mood, thought it would make a good picture and said so.

"Gross," said Angela.

"That's what I need," said Rollo, cupping his hands around his eyes and squinting through the glass at the prices. "Give Lance something to think about."

When they reached Gabriel's, Angela buzzed then stepped back into the street and shouted, "Yo, Gabe!" Presently an arm appeared and a key came arcing out the window. Angela snatched the key mid-air and a minute later they were riding the freight elevator up, a cage built of splintered two-by-eights smelling of cloves and cigarettes.

Gabriel was cranking a yellow plastic salad spinner when they entered. "The Canooks!" he shouted, his grin displaying newly bleached teeth. He was lean and tall and what remained of his thistly hair dangled in a frizzled ponytail tied with a black velvet ribbon. He sported a Seattle Mariners baseball shirt, a silver bracelet, a ruby ear stud, cream-coloured linen pants, and bare feet with alarmingly long toes. *"Mi shithouse es su* shithouse." Gabriel let go of the salad spinner and opened his arms wide, and Willie watched Angela hug and kiss him far longer than necessary — far, far longer. She broke off the embrace and made introductions.

Gabriel saw the battered state of Willie's face. He shook Willie's hand and gave it a sturdy squeeze. "So. Dad. Bit of a rough trip so far?"

Willie responded with a small smile, all that his split lip would allow. What was it about men and the handshake, the grip contest, the old flex and squeeze to settle the ever-lurking question of who would dominate? Thirty years in construction had, if nothing else, given Willie strong hands and he gave old Gabe a taste; Gabriel tried to keep up, but for all his gym work and tai chi and jogging he had neglected his grip, and so the two of them stood there, smiling, each trying to crush the other's metacarpals, Willie gradually, inexorably, amping up the pressure. "Gabriel. Good to meet you," he lied.

Gabriel was tenacious. He held on and tried going the distance. Mastering his pain, he gave Willie a wry look as if to say, *I know you're a lying bastard who hates my guts for humping your baby girl, but for the sake of goodwill we will maintain these facades, won't we?* Then he abruptly let go. Willie had won, but he grew forlorn over having given in to such a base contest.

Gabriel nodded to Rollo and Carmen, and reserved a big hug for Juliet, who he led to the window where he invited her to admire the view.

"Check out that light," he said.

"Did it yourself, did you?"

Of course, Grandma did not approve of him either. Gabriel plugged the gaping crevasse with laughter. The afternoon sunshine highlighted the red tones in the brick walls, warmed the wooden beams, and enriched the rugs. Willie knew that the red-cedar-slat Venetians must have cost Gabriel a fortune. The place had a twenty-foot ceiling, brick floor, massive fir beams, and windows wide enough to crane freight through. The obligatory herd of large fat flies wandered across the glass, buzzed furiously, then resumed their stumbling travels. What a twilight zone, thought Willie, their fly brains tormented. Down on the street, panhandlers were busy alongside junkies and fishmongers while an old man who looked like John Lee Hooker busked with an upright bass. A clutch of tourists waddled by dressed in geriatric-wear that struck Willie as indistinguishable from baby clothes. They skirted wide around a madman thrashing a bicycle with a blue suede cowboy boot. The window was open and Willie heard the madman beating time with the boot as he chanted: "Four . . . score . . . and . . . seven . . . years . . . ago . . ." Willie turned away and spotted a free-standing

Japanese screen painted with life-sized pornography — a samurai with a large forearm-sized penis entering a swooning geisha — and beyond it a futon patterned with koi and cherry blossoms. Willie nearly swooned himself with nausea imagining his little girl in there. Surely some law would see Gabriel pilloried.

Juliet detached herself from Gabriel's long-fingered grip and strolled about admiring the place, not so discreetly wiping her palms against each other as if they had been fouled by his touch, noting the air plants and a Moroccan wall hanging of camel hair and goat. The sunlight burned in the glass beads of her dreads and she looked admirably taut and tanned in her tight white T-shirt.

"Juliet lived in Mexico City," said Angela proudly.

"Where?"

"Hotel Oxford."

"Overlooking the park? The concierge with the voice?"

Juliet nodded and Gabriel crowed with delight. Angela stood with her hip cocked and a grin on her face as if to ask how cool was that? She now began making a performance of how at home she was. "Where's the Salif Keita?"

"Where you left it," said Gabriel, not looking at her.

"I left it here."

"Then it's there." Gabriel winked at Willie as if to say, you see what I put up with? His cheeks looked dry and sallow beneath the sparse grey fibres of his beard. A wiry guy. He probably did kung fu and knew some secret spot on your throat where he could paralyse you with a poke of the finger.

"We were just talking about these things," said Juliet, standing in front of a metre-high brass-bowled hookah with three tubes woven with silk and tipped with ivory mouthpieces.

"Picked that up in Fez."

Juliet rolled her eyes in recollection.

Gabriel cackled. "You were there?"

They discovered they'd been in Maroc within weeks of each other back in 1971. Gabriel began singing "Marrakech Express." Juliet, not quite so enthused, discovered an Oriental wall scroll of a robed and bearded warrior-sage about to draw his sword. "So this is what, your alter ego, the *you* you wish you were?"

Gabriel winced and moved on to, "Ridin' on that New Delhi freight train . . . Ridin' on that New Delhi line . . ." He hit a high and plaintive note, "And I'm lonesome all the time. . . ." Then he plunked a case of Piety Flats Syrah 2003 down on the butcher block and grinned displaying teeth that were as long as his toes. "Let's get pissed."

While the others drank and chatted, Willie made Rollo try Dwayne again. For the next hour he phoned half a dozen times with no luck. Angela's laughter grew more and more brittle and high-pitched. At one point she disappeared and returned wearing harem pants with a taut red spandex top that accentuated her nipples. Gabriel announced dinner and they sat down to broiled salmon, dry-fried seaweed, steamed beet greens and baby potatoes.

Gabriel turned to Angela and in his best Mick Jagger sang, "Ay-an-gee. I still love you. Could you bring the sa-lad *por favor?*"

Angela set the burl bowl in the middle of the knotty pine table. The placemats were weaved of some exotic grass and the salad forks carved of some equally exotic wood. Gabriel guided them through the salad. "Swiss chard, spinach, Italian 'rugula and cherry tahmaters. There's the walnut oil and the raspberry vinegar."

Before the apple pie arrived, Willie excused himself to the washroom where he rediscovered the simple and profound relief that came with elimination. He also discovered there was no toilet paper, only a wicker basket full of *Vanity Fair*. He finally dredged up a wadded napkin from his pocket, unfolded it carefully, pressed it flat on his thigh, and tore it into pieces. He then opened the medicine cabinet, a troublesome habit he seemed to be developing of late, swallowed three codeines and drank from the faucet. When he returned to the table Angela was eyeing him so strangely that Willie asked what was going on.

Gabriel cut in. "Sorry Willie, should've warned you. I don't believe in dry wiping."

"It's unsanitary," said Angela.

"Soap and water and . . ." Gabriel twiddled the fingers of his left hand in the air. "Cured my hemorrhoids in two weeks. Learned that in India," he added. "The wisdom of the East. What say we fire up that hookah?" Gabriel glanced hungrily at Angela, whose apologetic twitch of a shrug revealed to Willie a new dimension to her love affair. So. She was Gabriel's connection. That bag had been for him. Now Angela looked beseechingly at Willie: was he going to bring down the pall of Gabriel's disappointment over her head, was he going to fail her, let her down, now of all times? Along with his bad hair, short teeth, lumpy nose, and pitted complexion Willie had given Angela his insecurity, that grim little enzyme, that wobbly chromosome of self-doubt that made him buy approval and affection with money and labour and gifts.

༄

Willie made the trek to the Caddie where he unlocked the trunk, unzipped the backpack and peeled open one of the pound bags and then shoved a fistful of bud into the baggie that Angela had plucked from beneath Gabriel's sink. He was in a parking lot and worked quickly but casually, even as his mind raced ahead envisioning the news report of the Canadian in police custody in Seattle pending charges for importing a large quantity of marijuana. When Willie returned with the bag he found everyone reclining on cushions arranged around the hookah set in the middle of the carpet. He dropped the bag in the hookah's bowl and Gabriel made a savouring sound as if about to taste some succulent fruit. He plucked it up and opened it, tested a bud between his fingers and declared it a tad moist. Willie remained defiantly indifferent to this declaration and uttered not a word of explanation. Stepping into the kitchen, Gabriel spread the pot on a cookie sheet and slid it into the oven at a low heat. Angela's relief earned Willie a grateful smile which Willie did not return, and so Angela's gratitude devolved into a grimace of boredom.

Ravi Shankar graced them with a raga for the evening. The light deepened and the street shouts relented — Sunday, the city settling into a lull before the late-night revellers took over the stage. The thump of the bass-playing busker reached them like a pulse. "I gotta start school tomorrow," said Angela, sounding like an old workhorse returning to the plough. "Five classes. First day. God. Last semester I had homework on the first night!"

Wearing paisley oven mitts, Gabriel set the tray of dried pot on the stovetop and scrutinized it. "Fresh from mother Gabriel's kitchen." He poured it onto a plate and carried it like a fresh batch of brownies to the others seated on the rug. "So, Willie." Gabriel focussed on the task of crumbling bud into the hookah's brass bowl. "I understand you need a buyer for your crop."

Willie glanced at Angela, who had suddenly discovered a keen interest in the liner notes of the Ravi Shankar disc. Rollo didn't like the sound of this. He leaned closer, a frown darkening his face.

"It's just that I know a little old lady in Sausalito," crooned Gabriel. "She'd take it all." Gabriel snapped his fingers. "Like that. If it's good," he added, looking Willie in the eye.

The codeine was rising like warm mist and along with it Willie's confidence. He was angry with Angela yet prudent enough to listen. Rollo sat up tall and attentive; Carmen and Juliet raised their chins and narrowed their eyes. Willie said, "Judge for yourself."

"I intend to." All watched the ritual of Gabriel packing the pipe. He took up one of the silk-wrapped leads, struck a foot-long fireplace match and lit the pot and sucked. The smoke hubble-bubbled through the water in the lower chamber of bellied brass scribed with vine patterns. Gabriel had good wind; he made that water boil. He passed the lead to Juliet and then exhaled a cumulus of smoke. "Three thousand a pound."

"U.S.?"

"Only currency that counts."

Willie's mind whirred through the math. Three thousand U.S. was a good price. Seventy-five thousand U.S. dollars. His nerves flared like roman candles as possibilities loomed, yet he merely nodded noncommittally while the others regarded him with new respect.

"Not bad, this is not bad at all," Gabriel said of the smoke after his second pull on the pipe. "BC Bud. Who'd've thought the cheeseheads'd take over the market."

Rollo was trying to get Willie's attention. "Willie . . . Hey . . ."

Carmen put her arm around Willie. "More wine, baby?" She reached for the bottle and filled her man's glass. "You look tired." She turned to Gabriel. "We've had a tough couple of days. Willie's been through the mill." She knelt behind Willie and began massaging his neck. "Haven't you, baby. How you feeling? Glass of water? Are you drinking enough water?"

Rollo was blinking rapidly as if he might cry. "Look. Whoa. Hey. Hold on. Willie'n me, we got a deal underway."

Carmen snapped, "It flopped, Rollo. It died. The guy didn't show."

Rollo asked to use Gabriel's phone again. While he punched numbers and paced by the window, Carmen whispered, "Seventy-five thousand U.S. dollars, Willie." Her voice was husky with innuendo and yet so soft it might have come from within his own mind. Carmen looked to Gabriel. "We'd have to drive it down ourselves?"

"Be a nice drive," smiled Gabriel. "Oregon coast. Then the

redwoods."

Rollo continued pacing the far side of the room with the phone.

"Give it up, Rollo," called Carmen.

Rollo waved her off then put his finger in his ear. "Dwayne! Buddy! Hey. What happened, man? Where you been? Two days I been calling —"

Carmen strode to Rollo, pried the phone out of his startled grip, said, "Toodle-oo, Dwayne. Deal's off," then pressed the button and delivered the cell back to Gabriel. "You're just crying about your commission."

Rollo's arms hung limp as socks.

"Which does raise a point," Gabriel admitted.

"Hundred a pound," said Carmen.

"Willie, c'mon, man. You been living in my place —"

"For three grand a month!" shrieked Carmen. "We were robbed. Willie was beaten up. Your place is jinxed."

Gabriel was enjoying this. He looked to Willie. "So. Do I make the call?"

Carmen knelt in front of Willie and took his hands in hers and gazed into his eyes, indifferent to the others watching, for this was the point where the paths forked, this was the moment of decision, and she was not about to let it go unguided. "We could buy an orchard."

Seventy-five thousand U.S. dollars was about ninety or so Canadian; it was good but it would not buy an orchard, or not much of one. Still, it was a fine chunk of tax-free dough, and there had never been a moment of doubt as to what to do. He nodded to Gabriel. "Okay."

Carmen embraced him. Rollo groaned. Angela yipped in delight at the prospect of adventure. Juliet observed and kept her own counsel. Gabriel offered a ritualized bow and took the cordless into the other room, leaving them to wait in silence. Presently they heard Gabriel chattering and they strained to hear. The conversation proceeded *sotto voce* for a while. Willie's heart thumped so hard his vision quavered. Eventually Gabriel emerged from behind the screen and for a moment he stood there with the phone dangling from his thumb and forefinger. A floor lamp made of cedar and rice paper lit him from the side giving him a stark and craggy appearance, a man of light and shadow. "You like prawns?"

"Prawns?"

"We're invited to supper in Sausalito day after tomorrow. Baked tiger prawns with elephant garlic, oregano and butter."

Willie stood. "So we're set?"

"Set in stone." Gabriel strode across the room and extended his hand and this time their grips were all warmth and friendship.

Angela clapped and whistled and shook her fists over her head. "I've never been down through the redwood forest."

Gabriel turned to her, smiling politely. "What about your classes? Don't want to start off behind," he advised, suddenly pragmatic and wise.

Willie nodded. "I think you've gone far enough in this."

Betrayed, Angela's face twisted as she fought tears. "You bastards! You shits!" She stepped back as if they were assassins. The victorious Carmen stayed silent and let the others mop up while Rollo, solemn in loss, remained apart on the window ledge, watching the street and the lone bass-playing busker.

"Redwoods've been there a thousand years, baby," said Juliet. "They'll be there come Christmas holidays. We'll drive down then. You and me. Promise."

Angela turned from her and confronted Gabriel. "You just want to fuck her, don't you? You just want to fuck my grandmother, you pervert."

"Angie...."

"Oh, right, let's hear from Miss Beauty Bitch 1959. She's gonna take a lot of upkeep, Gabe." Angela began circling her grandmother as if sizing up a car in a lot. "First thing is new tits. Definitely need replacing. Too many miles. Then the face. Lotta work there. And don't forget to nip and tuck that tummy. I figure ten-fifteen grand and you can get her back on the road for one last ride —"

The slap resounded as sharply as shattered glass. Angela's hand rose to her stung cheek and her eyes flooded with tears as her lips trembled. Juliet's palm was scorched and her own face red with rage. Willie decided he'd give them both five thousand dollars when the deal went through.

CHAPTER 17

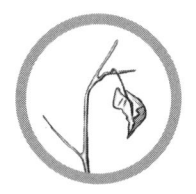

THEY DROVE SOUTH OUT OF Seattle past the Sea-Tac International Airport and on toward Oregon, Gabriel eventually directing Juliet off the I-5 to the more scenic coastal route. He had taken the seat up front, his freshly shampooed ponytail tied with a red leather lace. For the first hour of the journey the mood remained subdued. They'd eaten breakfast in a retro café featuring booths with jukeboxes where Gabriel had insisted on ordering a round of Bloody Marys, reminding them about the chlorophyll in celery and the benefits of moderate alcohol consumption on cholesterol. Angela had set her drink to one side as if it were toilet water and remained disdainfully silent the entire meal while Carmen crooned over her huevos rancheros. When they dropped Angela off at school, she slammed the door and walked away without a word, leaving Willie devastated. Her shoulders looked so thin and fragile. Fearing he'd never see her again, he put his hand on the door handle and began to open it to go after her but Juliet reached back and gripped his arm, her expression counselling him to stand firm. He opened the door anyway.

She gripped his arm tighter and gave it a shake. "Willie. Willie...."

Reluctantly he pulled the door shut.

Next they dropped an equally unhappy Rollo at the bus station. In an effort at salvaging what had been an abiding if not particularly honourable association, Willie became generous.

"Rollo. Take my van and everything in the house. There's ten grand worth of equipment in the basement." He dug in his pocket and detached his car key.

Rollo had accepted the reality of the situation. His commission was gone, and by the looks of it so was Willie and all that sweet rent. He shook hands with everyone.

"Rollo!" cried Carmen at the last moment, causing Willie a spasm of fear that she was going to declare her love, that she'd thought it all over and no money was worth losing him. Rollo turned. "Rollo, my pictures. Can you store them for me? Please?"

He gazed at her. Willie looked from Carmen to Rollo and back to Carmen again trying to read what, if anything, was passing between them.

"Sure," said Rollo, shrugging, his hands deep in his pockets. "Sure. If Lance doesn't break my knees." With that, he turned and trudged into the bus station and exile.

❧

Now the Caddie glided the coast road between farmland and sea, and Willie stared out the window.

Selecting his words as if composing an evaluation for a report card, Gabriel said, "Angela is as intelligent as she is intense. She will go far in her life. But," he added, never once turning to look at Willie in the back seat, "her road will not be a smooth one."

Gabriel had just broken his daughter's heart. A father of any honour would take old Gabe by the throat and start squeezing until he turned a few interesting shades of purple. But the fact was that he was glad they were split up, and assaulting Gabriel now would serve only to blow the deal.

Willie stared at Gabriel's tanned and vulnerable scalp visible through the thinning scrub. The remnants of Gabriel's hair gathered together in a ponytail put Willie in mind of the scorched arse of a rodent, and though he would rather not do so, his mind's eye began envisioning an anus on the back of the man's skull, an anus that now twitched to life and began swelling and pushing outward, expressing a dribble of excreta that ran down Gabriel's neck and into his collar. Willie shook the vision from his mind and thought of Angela making love to the man, felt crushed, briefly caught Juliet's eye in the rear-view, and turned away and looked out the window at the rich fields of high green grass levelling off to the dull glitter of the sea.

❧

The Caddie died just past Lincoln City. Gabriel's American Express Platinum Card got them a mechanic, a serene-looking man with an enormous iron crucifix around his neck and greasy overalls. His stitched name tag read Cal. Cal towed them back to his shop and opened the hood and leaned into the motor and admired it. "Engines were so simple in those days," he said with the nostalgia of an old rock 'n' roller disgusted with the state of contemporary music. He was about sixty-five and tattooed with skulls and demons and spiderwebs. He pulled on a pair of surgical gloves, lit up a Marlboro and leaned deeper into the motor, indifferent or oblivious to the fire hazard, the lit cigarette bobbing as he spoke sending little sparks tumbling about the machinery. "Alternator's fried." He led them into his office through a door with a McPherson struts calendar tacked onto it. In the corner was a bookstand and on it a white-covered Bible the size of a birthday cake. He lay his cigarette in an ashtray shaped like a baptismal font, consulted his computer, then swivelled the monitor so that they could see for themselves the costing display.

"Two hundred and ninety-nine dollars," read Gabriel.

Cal picked up his cigarette and savoured the last puff before stubbing it out. "You in a hurry? If you got a coupla' days I can hunt around the yards here, maybe find you a used one."

Willie and the others exchanged looks. Willie said, "I'll pay you back."

"Go ahead," said Gabriel.

Cal nodded and then became reflective, tipping his head and stroking his shaved cheek. "I know it's painful, but she's an old car and I would highly recommend a tune-up. I mean," he leaned to look through the office window at the licence plate. "British Columbia. Long drive."

"How long will it take you to get a new alternator?"

Cal cocked his head back and consulted the round white clock on the wall behind him. "Last delivery's at three. Got to come out from Salem. Have you on the road by five. Barring unforeseen complications of which there are often too many to avert or avoid."

But Cal was up to the task and they reached the Redwood National Park at sunset, the last of the light blazing high on the trunks. They drove on through the forest as dusk fell and reached Eureka under a starry sky and found a motel.

The desk clerk smiled and raised his arms as he told them the good news: there were two rooms left, just right for two happy couples. Juliet smiled thinly and stood a little more erect as she enquired as to the nature of the beds.

"Kings."

"Ah." Juliet's fingertips did a tentative tap dance on the edge of the counter. "Then we are very lucky indeed, aren't we," she said with a smile so dry her lips got caught on her teeth.

Carmen was rather disappointed that their rooms were not side by side. Willie failed to enter into the jolly spirit of voyeurism. "Oh, well," she said, inclined to be philosophical as she explored the room with the excitement that always overtook her in hotels and motels. She opened and closed the accordion doors of the closet and noted the crusty black scabs of cigarette burns on the rug. The clicker was held together with silver duct tape. She aimed it at the small TV perched on a wall bracket high in one corner. The screen rippled and opened its eye and

Carmen began ticking through the stations. She sat next to Willie on the side of the bed, and while continuing to surf took his hand and said, "Hey, grumpy boy. You should be glad. At least the guy's not with Angie anymore. Juliet's doing us all a favour." Carmen had regained the imperious tone of the victorious. She lingered a moment on a beauty pageant, girls in bathing suits and tiaras and spike heels, Miss Malagasy Republic, Miss Mauritius, and then moved on. "Rollo better take good care of my pictures. I better phone him. He's got to store them someplace clean and dry. But not too dry." She picked up the bedside phone and began an involved discussion with the desk clerk about long distance calls.

"Country code, area code and then the number. And you'll put it on the bill. Okay." Rollo didn't answer so she left a message then hung up and chewed her lower lip, and resumed clicking through the stations. Miss Sri Lanka, Miss Surinam, Miss Sierra Leone. She found a travel show on Costa Rica and turned up the volume. Then she opened the mini-bar and knelt before the assorted bottles, taking them out and turning them in the light as if admiring jewellery. "Look, tequila, we can warm up for Mexico." She glanced over her shoulder at Willie lying on the bed, nearly spread-eagle as if he'd fallen there from a great height. On TV, the tour guide was feeling road weary so he pulled his SUV into a quaint Costa Rican town, and the camera cut in close to watch a woman with the long smooth features of a bronze mask squeeze the juice of six large oranges into a glass while in the background a fly-covered sow of stupendous girth endured the suckling of a dozen voracious piglets, a spectacle frightening in its raw urgency.

Naked but for a T-shirt, Carmen appeared beside him holding two plastic cups. "Cheers, baby." She knocked her cup against his and sipped her drink. He drank his in one go as if it were water, and remembered that he hated tequila, that it tasted the way carpet cleaner smelled. They watched the tour guide canoeing along an emerald river beneath an arcade of leafy trees. "Hey," suddenly inspired, she began peeling off her T-shirt. "Wanna have a shower with me? Come on, Willie. Let's have a shower." Jiggly with excitement, her boobs bobbling, she grabbed his hand and pulled him to his feet. They made love in the shower and then fell asleep in each other's arms.

⁂

In the morning, Willie woke to Carmen drawing him.

"Don't move."

His back was to her. "I have to pee."

"Doesn't matter. Hold it." She was sitting cross-legged on the bed, sketching on a sheet of motel letterhead. "You're beautiful, Willie. Did you know that? The line from your neck to your shoulder. Wow. I never noticed. You know, that's the thing, I don't really see until I draw something. That's sad. Or maybe not. Maybe I should just draw more. Draw everything. I think Mexico is going to be good for us. I can feel it. I'm inspired already. All that light. It's good for the brain. Sunlight and colour. I'm going to get into colour. Get a studio. A show. And a camera. We need a camera. A good one. Digital. Did you sleep alright?"

"No."

"Okay. Done."

He rolled toward her and she showed him the drawing. It was mostly rucked and wrinkled blankets, but did include a rear view of his shoulder, neck and ear.

"I love your ears. I'm going to do a series on you. All through Mexico." She took the drawing back and began adding to it. "Mirrors are bad. Do you love me?"

"Of course." He went into the bathroom and studied his ears.

⁓

They ate at Smitty's and Willie experienced nothing short of wonder at the monumental size of the American breakfast — the waffles and hotcakes so large they loll over the edges of the platter-sized plates, the triple-yoked eggs, the obscene sausages, the lengths of fat-marbled bacon, the ice-cream scoop balls of butter, the sopping toast, the endless cups of soot-black coffee, the token wedge of orange, the micro-garnish of parsley — and he was nothing less than awed at the colossal size of Americans themselves, heifers and bulls splendid at their cud.

Gabriel picked at a fruit salad and appeared preoccupied, alternately frowning and sheepish, as if replaying some scenario in his mind. Had Juliet declined his advances? Had she treated him to a lecture? Or was it that Mr. Sport not been up to the task? Then again Willie wondered if Gabriel was enduring an attack of guilt at what he'd done to Angela. Willie was sure he was avoiding his eye. Willie glanced at Juliet, but she was demurely occupied with the *New York Times* crossword and a second cup of Earl Grey. When the bill came Gabriel took it and Willie reminded him to keep all the receipts.

That seemed to wake him up. "What? Oh. Sure." He smiled and sat back and placed his palms flat on the tabletop. "So, hey, coast road or 1-5?"

Juliet lay her arm like a warm scarf around his shoulders and put her face close to his. "Whatever you think, baby."

Gabriel could only stare, flustered, and blinking at this great cat of a creature.

Carmen went off to use the phone, and after more coffee and a leisurely amble out to the car, Willie went to get her because the others were growing impatient; he found her in a heated argument. He was too far away to hear the words, but he could clearly see by the way she gripped the receiver and drove her fingers through her hair that she was upset. When she spotted him approaching she reacted as if she'd been caught stealing and quickly hung up.

"Who was that?"

"Goddamn Rollo hasn't even been over to look at the place yet."

❧

By three that afternoon they were edging into the fringes of the greater Bay Area traffic. Smart Cars cut from lane to lane in and around Hummers and SUVs and Lincolns, as well as all the generic AMCs and Hondas. Gabriel pointed out the exit and soon they were winding their way up into the cobbled lanes of Sausalito past boutiques and cafes and villas. Willie gazed upon the bright sunny world of affluence while Gabriel navigated them through the streets. As they swung around a tight turn they met a squad of police cars blockading a house. A patrolman left the yellow crime tape and strode toward them with his palm extended, ordering them to halt.

Gabriel remained calm and pitched his voice low. "Don't worry. We're white."

Juliet stopped the car and rested her elbow on the window ledge and prepared to be charming. The cop bent to scrutinize them all, a handsome young Latino groomed to an almost painful perfection. "Licence and registration, please ma'am." As the cop checked Juliet's licence and registration, Gabriel affected an affable innocence. He leaned to see the crime scene and inquire as to what had happened.

"Triple homicide." The officer stepped back. "Okay, move on."

Juliet eased her foot down on the gas and the Caddie purred low in its throat and slid away.

"Up there." Gabriel indicated an apartment building of scalloped white masonry.

Juliet pulled in along the sidewalk and the spiral warning wire angling from the wheel well scraped the concrete. Close enough. She thrust the column shift into Park, gunned the gas one more time and switched off the ignition. Willie contrived a casual glance back and saw that the cop was still watching them.

"He's watching."

"Maybe he likes old cars," said Gabriel, getting out.

Juliet joined Willie at the trunk. She turned the key and the lid floated up. He leaned in and worked the pack free from beside the spare tire. Juliet leaned in with him. "Almost there," she said encouragingly.

He asked her how it was going.

"Fine," she said. "Just fine." Then she put her hand on his shoulder. "Hey. Don't worry. I know what I'm doing." They looked at each other and, for the first time they were equals. "And you?"

For a moment he was caught off guard and then realized she meant him and Carmen. "Okay. Good." Willie swung the pack to his shoulder and turned toward the apartment. Had he sounded more convincing than he felt?

Charlotte met them at the door. She was a seventy-year-old woman with a cape of grey hair that hung to her heels. Her hair made her appear gnomish, and it followed each of her movements with a slight delay, always a half step behind. Broad silver clips at her temples kept it clear of her lined face and she wore silver ear pendants. As if fearful of setting herself on fire, she held her gold-tipped cigarette out to her side as she stood on her toes to hug Gabriel. Then she led them up the steep stairs carpeted with a second-rate grade of indoor/outdoor, to her third floor suite. It was like following a human hay sheaf. The apartment was bright though smelled heavily of cigarettes, and was decorated with cheaply mounted black-and-white photos of sand: beach sand, desert sand, wind-sculpted dunes, raked sand gardens in Japanese temples. Afternoon sun blazed across the white walls and Willie noted that the floor was one-inch tongue-and-groove oak badly in need of refinishing. Charlotte was breathless after the hike up the stairs, and this added to her seemingly natural distraction as she ushered them to a sandstone-coloured couch.

She stepped to the sliding glass balcony door and checked the crime scene down the street. "I was just making tea. Shit, they're still there. Gabriel, do you remember Monty the cartoonist with the hearing aid who went to Berkeley? He died last week."

This seemed of some mild concern to Gabriel, who had established himself in the chair that matched the couch. "Monty?"

"I know, I couldn't believe it." She stood in the middle of the room with the sun angling through the foliage of her hair as if through dead, dry underbrush. The kettle began to sing. She turned, hair swirling around her, and said, "Oh," as if she'd never heard such a thing as a kettle, as if she were Alice at the Mad Hatter's tea party, and she hurried off into the kitchen. Gabriel followed and there was muted conversation. They emerged with Gabriel carrying a rosewood tray that he set on the smoked glass coffee table. Charlotte towed a rocking chair closer and sat down, her bare toes scarcely touching the floor.

"I love the light here." She shut her eyes and basked for a moment before remembering her hostess duties, but Gabriel was ahead of her and already pouring the tea, so she offered her cigarette box around. She did this with both hands, a gesture that was Japanese in deference. The box was tin and painted with a mosque and palm trees. *Abdullah: Genuine Turkish Tobacco. Gold-tipped cigarettes.* Everyone declined the cigarettes except Carmen, who peered into the box as if at rare Belgian chocolates, and did not even glance guiltily at Willie as she took one. Charlotte took a cigarette as well, tapped it against a translucent knuckle, a gesture both worldly and nervous, then leaned toward the silver lighter on the coffee table in the shape of Napoleon on a horse. With a rich click the flame stood like a burning plume atop the forefinger of the emperor's raised right hand as if he were carrying a torch. Viewed up close, Charlotte's eyes were red and inflamed, the lids hung like bunched drapery, and her lips were dry. She sat back, holding her cigarette as if it were made of ornamental glass, and puffed delicately as though blowing farewell kisses. Her hair enclosed her, giving the impression of a life-sized doll that had been packed for shipping. After smoking a while she seemed ready to conduct business.

Everyone gathered closer as Willie unsealed one of the pounds. What a long time since he had packed them in Rollo's basement. His beauties had been through much. Charlotte chose a bud with one racoonish hand and sniffed at it as if appraising cheese.

"It's good," Gabriel assured her. "A touch damp, but very good."

"Did you hear that Penelope Glass has lesions?"

"No. We don't talk. Jerry still thinks I —"

"Oh, I know. He has so many issues." She dismissed Jerry with the hand that was holding the cigarette, scattering a trail of ash like a small comet.

"They were always —"

"It's true," said Charlotte. "Ever since the monastery." She took another sniff of the pot. "It smells good."

"It is good."

She returned the bud to the open bag and sat back and smoked her cigarette. The way she held it so still in her upraised hand gave the impression that her arm was a prosthetic locked into position. She looked off toward the sliding glass doors, turning her face full to the early evening sunlight that had altered and taken on a slightly crimson tone. "The son killed his parents and then himself."

Gabriel was the first to catch on. "Down the street . . ."

"With a hammer."

"He killed himself with a hammer?"

"No, I think he sucked the exhaust pipe of his dad's car. Or no, slit his wrists. That's right, he slit his wrists. Then he sucked the exhaust pipe. I don't care what they say it's just not the same anymore." She sounded forlorn and bitter and consoled herself with her cigarette, making a faintly sexual *mmm . . . mmm . . .* as she sucked wetly at the filter.

Gabriel's gaze circled the group, appealing to them all for patience. A day in the car had lent his complexion an oily sheen like something wrapped in cellophane. "So," he said, gently returning Charlotte to the business at hand.

She took his cue, ground her cigarette into the ashtray then got up and left the room, her hair floating out behind her, and returned with a small rattan sewing basket and a laptop that resembled a slab of slate. She set the basket on the coffee table and rotated it so that when she lifted the lid the others saw the contents first. Money. Everyone leaned in close, eyes widening and then narrowing as if to examine a small but alarming snake or a religious relic, the ear or tongue of a saint. There were Japanese yen, Mexican pesos, Singapore dollars, Irish pounds, U.S. and Canadian dollars.

"I thought it'd be all American," said Willie.

Charlotte plugged in the laptop and pressed the power button and it immediately began to hum. "It is mostly American." She spoke without guile or urgency but with the professional calm of a gallery guide. "We'll get today's rates. You can convert it downtown. There're currency brokers everywhere. Or the banks. They'll do it. They always need it for the tourists."

Willie picked out the bundle of pesos, the notes grubby and limp with use, pungent as only money can be with the combined smells of grime and paper and ink.

"We'll need pesos," said Carmen, taking them from him, mightily impressed by the weight of the wad of bills in her hand.

Willie examined the yen, the imperial palace, the emperor, then moved on to the Irish pounds and the Singapore dollars, the stock coarse between his fingers, the very weight of the money whispering in his ear of purchasing power. Money. Cash. Loot. He could feel the crackle of Carmen's excitement. He'd have to convert it all to traveller's cheques and arrange for a safety deposit box.

Charlotte was on-line now checking the Bank of America rates. She'd shifted her chair and the laptop so that they could all see the screen's luminous pulsing membrane. The manner in which the digits slid and subsided made Willie suspect that the screen would groan luxuriously if he were to stroke its throbbing surface. She moved from currency to currency, counting out the bills, wrapping the bundles in elastic bands, rewrapping the remainder. "I like to keep a range of currency on hand," she said. "We'll check the rates again in the morning and then you can go downtown and get it converted into whatever you want. Raymond wants to come by tonight for three pounds, and I think Oliver. He's taking five up to Tahoe. You remember Oliver? Just retired from Wal-Mart."

"*Wal-Mart.*"

Charlotte sighed at the indignity. They contemplated the terrible fact that their glorious youth was flown, the summer of love a distant and unreliable memory, their friends cancerous, compromised, or dead. Charlotte signed off and the screen purred and went to sleep as she closed the lid.

"*Bueno.*" Gabriel slapped Willie's knee, stood and stretched and then extended his hand to Juliet, who took a moment to observe him first, as if she had not seen him from this angle before and would like to evaluate him, and then finally she took his hand and together they strolled out onto the balcony.

"So, you're Canadian," said Charlotte.

"That's right."

And with that she lost interest.

❧

By noon the next day Willie had all the traveller's cheques he needed, Thomas Cook, American Express, Bank of America, plus twenty thousand he'd kept aside in U.S. cash and Mexican pesos. They hit a travel agency and got two tickets to Guadalajara for a flight departing the next afternoon. Willie gave Carmen and Juliet a thousand dollars each to pick up some clothes, then settled up with Gabriel, who led Willie around the corner for a couple of Anchor Steams and what would have been some awkward conversation had Gabriel not been set upon by an old pal, a character actor Willie recognized but couldn't name, a guy who always played detectives on the make or eastern European assassins who ended up being shoved off trains. Off camera, he looked twenty years older and thirty pounds heavier, and was downing double Jacks with a hiss and a grimace, and growing louder and more bitter at each gulp, glaring balefully at the door each time it opened as if expecting someone, as if fearing someone, and declaring that he hated everyone in this place, in this city, in this goddamn industry.

When Willie and Gabriel escaped back out into the San Francisco dusk, they hopped a cab and were soon speeding across the Golden Gate Bridge back to Charlotte's where they discovered Juliet modelling a new brassiere. An impressive sight it was. She turned when they entered and let them admire it, raising her arms and doing a slow pirouette while Charlotte flitted around her like some mad seamstress, cooing and nodding.

"What do you think, Willie?"

"Wow."

"Four hundred and eighty-nine bucks," said Carmen, her tone expressing a combination of awe and envy and disapproval at such extravagance.

"It's French," said Juliet.

Gabriel whistled.

Carmen informed Willie that she'd made reservations at the Hotel Francés, Guadalajara's oldest hotel. Both Juliet and Gabriel observed that it was a good choice.

The next morning they had breakfast in the Haight at a café that featured white pepper chai lattes with clarified buffalo milk and three-bean chili vindaloo. Willie breathed deep to calm his nerves. Events were racing ahead, and he was beginning to feel as if the money and the deal were in control, not him. Before leaving the café, he passed Juliet an envelope containing five thousand dollars. She slipped it into her bag and murmured thank you. They stepped outside and Gabriel excused himself saying he had some business to deal with and, hugging both Willie and Carmen a fond *adios*, arranged to hook up with Juliet later. Juliet then drove them out to San Francisco International and accompanied them into the terminal for a last farewell.

Carmen was done up in cotton and straw, a wide-brimmed beach hat with an artfully frayed brim that matched her shoulder bag, sandals and belt. Her silver toenails flashed like new dimes and her smile was so wide Willie feared her lips would split. A female voice announced the arrival of flights from Chicago and New York and departures for Manila and Singapore. The crowd flowed in conflicting currents with the occasional clash of luggage carts. Cops patrolled in pairs. Kids squealed and ran. Families hugged before the departure gates while a janitor pushing a mop travelled nowhere but across the darkly burnished floor. The lineups were formidable.

"See," said Carmen. "Aren't you glad we upgraded to first class?" She'd spent forty minutes on the phone that morning making the change, and now she led the way to the first-class check-in as if she were arriving at the opening of her show at the Tate. Propping her sunglasses atop the crown of her hat, she turned. "We're gonna have to pay the diff now, Willie. Can you give me some cash?"

"Sure." He was carrying a tan linen sportcoat slung over his forearm the way a waiter might carry a cloth. In the inside pocket waited an envelope. He handed it to Carmen. It was thicker than the thirty-dollar Argentinean steak she'd moaned over last night.

She looked at it and then at him. "Willie . . ." she said, as if he'd presented her with a diamond engagement ring set in platinum. Then she repeated his name, questioningly this time, her tone different, gravely different. "Willie?"

He took a step back. "That's your cut. Twenty thousand." Then he added, reminding her, "You've got your ticket. You'll be fine."

"Willie."

He turned and walked away.

"Willie . . ." Her voice reached out like an arm groping from rising floodwater.

He flinched but kept his gaze on the exit sign and his concentration on the female voice announcing the arrival of a Japan Airlines flight from Tokyo. Was she crying? He kept walking. Everyone was flowing past him the other way, as if he was pushing upstream. Once outside he was tempted to glance back, but unlike Orpheus he did not give in.

"Willie." Juliet stood next to him, watching to see how he was holding up. She placed her hand on his shoulder and gave a reassuring squeeze. "When did you decide?"

"I don't know." He looked up. The sun was hot and dry and had blanched the sky to the colour of sidewalk cement. He lowered his gaze. The light flared off the hoods of Mercedes and limousines. Finally he looked down at his feet, clad in a pair of huarache sandals Carmen had picked up for him yesterday along with the linen sportcoat.

"Too bad about the ticket," remarked Juliet.

He took it out of his shirt pocket. "Want it?"

She plucked it like a card from a deck then fluttered it like a fan.

"Does he know?" he asked.

"If he has any brains he does."

"It'll be a long flight next to Carmen."

Eyes narrowed against the glare, she said, "I'm sure they'll let me downgrade to economy." She dug in her pocket and dangled the keys to the Cadillac. "I know you'll take good care of her. You've always been good to me. Too good, maybe."

Willie blew a long puff of air, and observed the comings and goings of the people around them, the whirr of suitcase wheels, the thump of car doors, the laughter and shouts. They heard the final call for the flight to Guadalajara. "What'll you do," he asked her, "look up old friends?"

A smile tickled her lips. "Maybe a new one."

It took Willie a moment. "Not Ed?"

She pretended to be offended. "He's not *that* bad." She waved the plane ticket as if savouring its scent and then winked. "Maybe I can get in his will." After one last hug she looked him in the eye. "Check the road map," she said. "There's one in the glove compartment. You don't want to make any wrong turns."

"What do you mean?"

"Just do it."

CHAPTER 18

THERE WAS A BAG OF POT UNDER the road map in the glovebox, a big bag, three or maybe four ounces, a quarter pound of bud. Gabriel's idea? Willie got out and stashed it in the trunk and then got back in behind the wheel and fit the key in the ignition. He was frightened but it felt exhilarating to be alone. He pulled out, and soon the scream of the jetliners landing and taking off was behind him.

He drove north, and by eight that evening reached Eureka where he stopped at the same motel and phoned Angela who promptly informed him she'd quit school. He sighed long and hard but didn't ask why. The next evening, not far from Gabriel's loft, they sat in a restaurant overlooking Elliot Bay. Her face was as hard as a walnut as she sipped a pint of India

Pale Ale. Willie asked if she would go overseas again.

She shrugged. "Mom offered to pay my way down to Buenos Aires." Angela noted her father's lack of enthusiasm. "Her boyfriend Oscar's rich. I could work in his bar. He's got, like, five of them."

The restaurant was done up in fishing gear, the ceiling webbed with a net weighted with glass floats. She swung her sullen gaze back to her father and, in a voice as acrid as cut onions, asked, "So, how are the lovely couple? One big geriatric honeymoon? They can probably get a cut-rate on His-and-Her facelifts." Yet her bitter tone was contrasted by the desperation in her eyes. *Please*, they said, *contradict me, did Gabriel break down and weep and call my name?*

Willie was glad to be able to give her the news. "Grandma gave him the slip. Vamoosed on down to Mexico. Same flight as Carmen," he added, thinking she'd enjoy that.

"*Juliet and Carmen?* Oh, God, I didn't think they made planes big enough." Then Angela quickly reclaimed her anger and went on the offensive. "I guess that's supposed to make me feel better, right?"

"It should."

She briefly met his gaze then her glance skated away, furtive and uncertain. "And you?"

Willie knew the question was an afterthought, a politeness to fill the silence. He sat back and considered the nautical charts resin-sealed onto the cedar-plank table and all those swirling lines. No, you were not your child's friend, you were their parent, a very different thing, and only when Angela herself had a child would she understand. "How are you off for money?"

She became even glummer. "Broke."

He gave her the envelope he'd prepared beforehand with five thousand dollars. She put on a half-hearted performance of being guilty at taking it, and for the rest of the evening they discussed politics until she said he must be exhausted. They went back to her place and Willie slept on the couch.

The next morning he continued north intending to cross the border. But then what? Lance? Rollo? Home? There was no home. He wanted to see Diane and apologize again, to be sure she was okay. Maybe he'd just phone, but he didn't even know her last name. When he reached Blaine, just ten minutes from her place, he drove around the town for a while to think things over and then parked on the main street and sat there, drumming his fingers on the red steering wheel and watching the tourists come in and out of the shops. A summer day in the northwest, a deep blue sky, a few white clouds, the air heavy with the low-tide scent of mud and seawater. Off to his left stood the rotting brown piles of an abandoned wharf, each one topped by a seagull. There was the hull of a beached fishing boat and, in the distance, the San Juan Islands and further on, beyond the imaginary line of the 49th parallel, the hazy outlines of British Columbia's Gulf Islands. He reached to pluck the key from the ignition but his hand dropped back into his lap. He deflated into the seat, shut his eyes and hated himself. Fifty years old. He rolled his head side to side and wished for someone to slap him. So what, she had an orchard. And so what, he had a whack of dough. No. It was stupid. Besides, she hated him, and for good reason.

With a sudden grunt of self-disgust he pulled the key from

the ignition, got out of the car and locked it. He needed to walk. As he passed the Seaview porn theatre, the doors swung open and Willie found himself reunited with Steve. From behind Steve stepped Clara and Myron. For a moment they all stared. Then Steve smiled and opened his arms as if to embrace him, and for an instant Willie thought it was okay, they could share a laugh over old times, former adversaries wizened by age and experience who were now comrades. But Clara and Myron were already moving crabwise to corral him. Willie stepped back and bumped into a parked car and Steve, arms still wide, advanced upon him and caught him up in a bear hug and spoke in his ear, the same ear into which he'd driven his railway-spike forefinger: "Shout and I'll crush your ribs." Demonstrating, he gave Willie a squeeze that popped every vertebra in his spine.

※

Steve liked the Cadillac. Elbow resting on the window ledge, he steered with his left forefinger while letting his right arm lounge out along the top of the seat back. He had not shaved his head or face in some days, and a dark whiskering of hair had grown in, betraying his male pattern baldness while his chin looked stubbled with iron filings. In the heat of the summer afternoon he bore about him a sturdy odour. And he was happy, travelling out along the country roads east of Blaine as if on an afternoon drive. "What did I tell you?" Steve was saying. "You have to be a spider. A spider is patient. He waits. I tell you, you go out in the morning. Early morning. Take a walk in the forest. What do you see? You see spiderweb, everywhere spiderweb. Very beautiful with the sun coming through. Like lace. My mother made lace. The best." Steve kissed his fingers. "The spider is a very successful bug. It will inherit the earth." Steve paused in his lecture to lean and gob out the window. Willie was seated in the back with Clara who had exchanged her baseball bat for a Hot Shot HS36 Cattle Prod. She'd already given three demonstrations, and Willie now cringed in the corner, his calf burnt right through his pants, the aftershocks still jolting him in muscle-cramping shivers that made him fear for his heart.

Myron, seated up front, had had enough of waiting. "How about here," he kept saying. "Or down there." Unlike Steve, Myron was shaved and wore cologne that smelled like gin. In an eerie coincidence, Clara wore a Seattle Mariners baseball jersey just like Gabriel's. Her Amazon hair was wild around her head and she was smiling. A big woman with a square chin and hard eyes, she sat with one foot up on the seat, the cattle prod resting on her knee, half turned toward Willie in case he tried something foolish.

"How about it farm boy?" Steve caught Willie's eye in the rear-view.

Clara, cold-eyed as a crocodile, leaned toward Willie and waved the yard-long barrel of the prod in front of his crotch and prepared to jab him. At the last instant she missed him on purpose and jolted the leather-panelled door. She yipped with glee. The car's door and ceiling bore half a dozen similar imprints.

"Watch it with that fucking thing," shouted Myron.

Clara swivelled and taunted Myron, threatening him while he sat as far up against the dashboard as he could. "You fuckin' crazy cunt!"

"Clara." Steve clucked his tongue. Then he addressed Willie. "My friend," he counselled in a voice husky with wisdom. "It's only money."

Willie tried to talk but his throat muscles were in spasm and he was having difficulty breathing. He opened his mouth but no sound emerged but a choked hack. When he tried to point, his arm refused to function. He shut his eyes and gave in to a spasm of trembling that wracked his entire body.

"He needs another one."

"Clara. Enough." Steve found a dirt road that suited him, pulled off in behind some walnut trees and blackberry bushes and switched off the motor. As the dust caught up and rolled over the Cadillac, Steve turned and, sighing long through his moustache, regarded Willie with the medieval solemnity of an icon. "He's fucked up. You are fucked up, aren't you, my friend?"

Clara grew defensive. "He didn't talk."

"Yeah, well, whataya fuckin' expect with you stickin' him with that thing, eh?"

Clara blew Myron a kiss.

Steve reached and pulled the trunk release. "Myron."

Myron all too happily got out, and soon they heard him rummaging.

Willie had contemplated many ways to handle the money. He'd thought of taping it to his torso, of prying open the door panel and slipping it inside, of putting it in the rocker panels the way they did in *The French Connection*. He'd also thought of packaging it up and mailing it, yet who would he mail it to? Rollo?

Steve tugged up the sleeves of his shirt and flexed his hands as if readying them for work. He leaned over the seat back, forefinger poised like a pistol barrel. What a square wrist he had. The handlebars of his moustache were frayed and matted, and a chilling blankness had spread across his eyes, a blankness that told of a man capable of torture, a man capable of forgetting all mercy and for whom violence was an essential life skill.

Myron now stuck his head in the front passenger side window. "No money. But I found this." He held up the bag of dope.

Steve received both these pieces of information without expression and without shifting his gaze from Willie. His eyes darkened and grew heavier, as if he were shifting to a more primeval plane of existence to better facilitate what he now had to do. He thickly cleared his throat. "Hold him."

But before Clara could move, Willie said, "The Kleenex box," the words stuttering epileptic from his lips.

Steve, Clara and Myron looked at each other, and then simultaneously turned to the daisy-patterned tissue box on the ledge behind the rear seat. Clara held the cattle prod under her arm and grabbed the box and tore it apart like a kid attacking a birthday present. Tissue snowed about the back seat. When Clara discovered the money she grinned like a girl who'd got exactly what she'd asked for. Myron chimed in with some buoyant foulness of his own. Then Clara's face fell as she held up not cash but traveller's cheques.

"Now what?"

Steve merely slid his gaze from the neatly bundled cheques to Willie and then back to the cheques. A bird sang in the walnut tree beside them and in the distance a trucker geared down. The windows were open but the car was stifling and the red interior cast a hellish atmosphere over the scene lending a

Satanic glow to Steve's olive complexion. Steve reached to give Willie a fond slap on the face then laughed and started the Caddie, backed out, turned around and proceeded at a leisurely speed back the way they'd come. "I would have done the same thing," said Steve. "Only an idiot runs around with so much cash. Clara, Myron: count."

The air flowing in cooled them all. It was Saturday, a lazy summer Saturday afternoon. Clara sang Pink Floyd as she counted, "Money!"

"*Fermé* your *bouche*, baby," said Myron, who then announced, "Twenty-six thousand, seven hundred."

"Thirteen thousand, two hundred, and forty," said Clara.

"For a grand total of —" Myron concentrated.

"Thirty-nine thousand, nine hundred, and forty," said Steve.

Myron crowed while Clara began strumming a tune on her cattle prod and leaning toward Willie as if to serenade him, her breath smelling of coffee and cherry Chiclets. They drove for a quarter of an hour along straight narrow roads, passing fields and orchards, barbed wire fences overgrown with blackberries, an old Chev abandoned in a pasture with the grass growing up through its windshield. They saw a collapsing barn grown grey from decades of weather, and they saw a hawk take flight from a carcass in a ditch.

"That's what I want," said Myron. "A hawk." He held up his forearm like a perch. "Like that Roxy Music cover. The guy with the helmet. A knight. Looking out over a misty field. . . ." Myron's head began to move forward and back, leading with the chin, as if he were riding a horse through a medieval vale.

"It's cruel," said Clara.

"They're not in cages."

"It's against the law."

"Aw, gee, no, is that right? I forgot you were such a stand-up citizen."

All the while the Caddie's fat tires hummed over the tarmac and Clara strummed her cattle prod and Myron spoke longingly of raptors. They reached Blaine and parked.

Steve checked his watch, the silver expansion bracelet stretched wide around his brick-thick wrist. "Just enough time to catch one bank before it closes." Gripping Willie's elbow, Steve walked him from the car to the bank entrance, coaching him as they went. "You don't look around. You don't talk. You go to the teller and do business. Cash cheques. Five thousand dollars. Then turn around and come out."

As Willie obediently nodded he also looked pleadingly at everyone who passed them on the sidewalk, trying to communicate his desperation with his eyes. There were elderly couples in beige and blue, young mothers pushing prams, lean men in western shirts, cowboy hats and boots, a very large man with orange hair and a chihuahua cradled in each arm. None looked at Willie much less grasped what was happening. Or, seeing all too well, they averted their eyes and hurried on by.

At the bank entrance, Steve sank his fingers like shark jaws into Willie's flesh in a foretaste of the agony that waited should he blow the whistle. "I'll find you, farm boy. I'll find you. And I promise you would wish you were torn apart by dogs instead." He paused to let the threat's full horror permeate Willie's imagination. Then he put his palm to his back and shoved him. "Go."

Inside the bank, Willie wiped at the tears that had spurted from his eyes at the pain in his elbow. He spotted an armed guard, spindly and arthritic, propped on a stool by a potted plant, reading a copy of *National Geographic* magazine. He joined the queue and waited his turn. Steve had given him one $5000 flap of cheques. Willie feared that between his crippled elbow and his trembling fingers he wouldn't be able to sign them. Or that he'd tremble so badly the teller would get suspicious. The line inched ahead, the tellers taking the customers one by one, making small talk, discussing the weather, the weekend. Finally, he was up next.

Which teller would he get? There were two middle-aged women and one guy. Did he dare lean across and whisper: *Please call the police. There are three people outside threatening to mug me.* A teller opened — the guy — but Willie didn't move.

His ears had begun to buzz as if he was about to pass out. The buzz grew louder and he felt ill. He'd never passed out in his life but somehow he was sure this was how it started. The teller looked questioningly at him, his mouth moving but no sound reaching Willie. The person behind him in the line tapped his shoulder and pointed. Willie launched himself forward and made it to the counter and leaned there, clinging, thinking he might vomit. What should he do? How could that old security guard help? Steve would crush him like a cracker. He took a deep breath, mastered his nerve-wracked wrist and began signing ten $500 cheques. He focused on his signature: Willie LeMat. What would a handwriting analyst make of the letters that were alternately jagged and wobbly? No, he wouldn't plunge down that path for it surely led to morbid self-disparagement. When he was done, the teller said something that Willie did not understand because he did not hear it. His ears didn't seem to be functioning, all he heard was a crackly static, as if his mind was a radio stuck between stations. The teller went away and stood at a machine. The machine blinked its lights, time passed, and Willie's heart thumped thick in his throat. Then money came ticking out of a slot, the bills landing one atop the other in a neat little pile, and the teller returned and counted them out to Willie. And with that, Willie was walking toward the glass door which the smiling security guard was holding open for him.

"Have a nice day," said the old man.

"You too," said Willie.

❧

They headed south to Bellingham. Steve took the Caddie; Clara and Myron drove the Econoline. Willie, having had another taste of the cattle prod, slumped twitching in the back of the van. They checked into a motel and divided up the five thousand. Myron was sent out for beer and pizza and duct tape. When he got back they wrapped Willie tighter than a mummy. "Big day tomorrow, farm boy. A lot more banking to do." Steve clouted him heartily on the back then shoved him into the closet and rattled the folding door shut. For a long time Willie did not move, just lay there listening to their talk and monitoring the state of his injuries. Bruises and burns mostly. Between the cattle prod and being slapped about, he ached all over but judged himself not too bad, or perhaps he was getting used to this perpetually mauled state; he was scared though, and worried he might foul himself. The door was slatted so that he could see their feet as they moved about the room on the indoor-outdoor carpeting that was worn to a shine. Soon he smelled pot. The TV was on the porn station and by the sounds of it Myron was talking on the phone. Clara was dispatched on another liquor run. Eventually there was a knock at the door and some women arrived, their voices piping and squealing in the false tones of call girls feigning delight in their work. Willie stayed very still, eyes wide, as frightened as he was fascinated. The evening started amiably enough, until someone said something and there was a slap and then the thump of a body hitting a wall. This was followed by a woman swearing at Clara and her fucking goddamn cattle prod, and how would she like it stuck up her ass? A bottle broke. Then everyone was swearing and then everyone fell silent.

"Steve. . . . Steve. . . ."

It was Clara, pleading. One of the women was whimpering, and Myron was trying to counsel calm. "Steve, hey, c'mon, man."

This was followed by a choked gurgling sound, like a pig having its throat slit. One of the women began to wail. The closet door was wrenched open and a girl shoved inside. Not seeing Willie, she shrieked and flailed thinking she'd landed on a corpse, while Willie curled into the fetal position to protect himself. The door rattled open again, and Myron and a naked woman with no pubic hair dragged her back out. In the few seconds the door was open, the bald-pussied woman and Willie made eye contact, but her gunmetal gaze plainly stated that no help was forthcoming, not from her, it was all part of the territory, and if he was taped up in a closet he probably deserved it, and besides she had seen worse. In the background, he spotted a frowning Clara seated crosslegged on the bed trying to repair the business end of her cattle prod.

He slept. He even dreamed. He was walking barefoot in an orchard on a summer morning. The branches were drooping under the weight of the fruit. The birds were chirping and there was a woman up ahead waiting for him. Willie felt relaxed and happy until the folding doors clattered apart and he woke to find Steve standing there, his bare chest covered with scores of butterfly tattoos of all sizes and colours, red and yellow and green and blue. His chest was thickly haired so that the butterflies appeared to be flying through forest. "Okay, farm boy." Steve hoisted Willie to his feet, stripped the tape from his hands and mouth and then propelled him toward the toilet. "Do what you have to do."

When Willie emerged Steve handed him an Egg McMuffin and a coffee. Willie couldn't eat so Steve shrugged and taped him back up and, with an usher's gesture, invited him to return to his closet. It was Sunday, and all morning and all through the midday Willie sat there in the slatted half light overhearing the TV, wrestling, baseball, porn, more wrestling, more baseball, more porn, reruns of *I Spy* — Willie had always liked *I Spy* — news, reruns of *Seinfeld* and *Frasier*. In the late afternoon he was permitted another visit to the bathroom and again offered the Egg McMuffin and the coffee. Too anxious to eat, he declined, drank some water from the faucet and returned to the familiar confines of his closet. It was a distinct disappointment to him that, at such a time, in such a crisis, he had no profound thoughts, no insights or revelations, he merely sat there smelling the acrid stink of his own fear, rerunning the same regrets in his mind, waiting for the seconds and the minutes to pass, and monitoring the mood in the other room. In the evening the doors opened and Steve handed him a bottle of Miller. Willie gratefully drank it down and Steve, amused, gave him another, and then a third; nerves dulled, Willie dozed.

Monday morning the doors opened, Steve stripped off all the tape and ordered him to take off his clothes. "What size are you?"

"Size?"

"Shirt, pants, what size?"

"Medium. Thirty-four waist, thirty-four leg."

The bathroom door opened and Clara emerged from the steam with a towel around her torso and one turban-wise about her head. Steve jerked his thumb toward the bathroom. "Shower. Shave."

Willie leaned against the shower wall with the hot water beating down on him, and struggled to gather his mind. They wouldn't hurt him, not now, not yet, not until they had the money, and even then there was no reason other than pure sadistic joy. But he didn't think that Steve was a sadist, no, he was reasonable — he was, sort of, he had a child, he'd bought diapers for it, Mars bars. Still, Willie thought of Lance and the others sitting on that slick of blood. He groaned. At five thousand a turn, it was going to take seven more banks to cash all the remaining cheques. There was a pounding on the door meaning hurry up. He turned off the water. All the towels were soaked, only a washcloth remaining untouched. He did the best he could with it and when he got out of the bathroom he found a fresh Egg McMuffin, an orange juice and a coffee awaiting him, plus a pair of no-name blue jeans, and a red-and-blue checked button-down shirt still in the plastic. He was too anxious for coffee, couldn't stomach McDonald's, so drank the juice, and tried not to whimper.

Willie accompanied Steve in the Caddie while Clara and Myron followed in the van, proceeding slowly through the streets of downtown Bellingham, a city that smelled of sausage and smoke. Willie was sweating with fear, and that caused the polyester shirt, a bargain bin throwback the texture of linoleum, to stink. They parked one behind the other a block down from a Bank of America. Steve turned to him, that feral expression dimming his eyes once again. He pointed his finger: the meaning was clear.

The security guard in this one was young and fit and clearly regarded his job as a grave responsibility, seeing it perhaps as the first step en route to becoming a police officer, a bodyguard or a secret-service agent. He studied Willie as he entered, eyes frisking him from top to bottom, warning him not to try anything. There was much chatter in the bank. Folks were feeling chipper, helping themselves to the complimentary coffee and gingersnaps off to one side. Willie joined the line behind an elderly lady leaning on a walker, her entire body trembling as if her idle needed adjusting. Her scalp, clearly visible through the fine fuzz of her hair, was as pale as parchment. Willie found himself gazing at it, wondering about her skull and her brain, and what dreams she had dreamed last night. Weak with anxiety, he wished he had a walker of his own to lean on. All too soon, he stood at the front of the line. He glanced back at the security guard who had his thumbs hooked into his black belt, the right one almost caressing his holstered pistol. He wore his hair in a crewcut and his eyes narrowed with a knowing expression as if he was not merely ready but hoping for action. The teller's green light signalled Willie's turn. He crossed the shiny linoleum with his cheques and his wallet and rested his elbows on the counter and looked the teller in the eyes. So, here he was again, pulse pounding like a pneumatic hammer hard enough to drive a spike through a plank.

The teller was a young woman with an Afro and a dark complexion. She smiled. "Holiday?" she asked, noting the cheques.

Images pinwheeled through Willie's mind: the butterflies snagged and dying in the hair covering Steve's chest, Clara jabbing Willie with that cattle prod, Rollo and Carmen reaching an orgasm together in the Johnny Canuck, Angela shooting heroin in Bangkok, his crop of marijuana — his babies — hacked down and stuffed into bags, Steve driving his finger into his ear, Steve hoisting him up and ramming him into the ceiling. Willie thought of all the mornings — winter, spring, summer and autumn — that he'd stood in a half-finished house, sipping a cup of coffee and admiring the play of the shadows through the framing, inhaling the spiced scent of fresh fir two-by-fours. Was Carmen right, should he have gone back into construction? Oh, God, Carmen. He could be with her right now in the Hotel Francés in Guadalajara, one of the oldest hotels in Mexico, a landmark, having breakfast, huevos rancheros, fresh juice, rich coffee, and planning another relaxing day of sightseeing, maybe an amble through the *mercado*, maybe an art gallery, then an afternoon of love and a siesta, followed by drinks on some tile-decorated patio. Instead he was here. The acid of humiliation mixed with the bile of rage burned his throat until his eyes watered. He would sign the cheques, and meekly follow the day through to its grim conclusion that would see him standing on the street, bruised, bleeding, broke and alone.

"Sir?"

Willie reached across the counter and gripped the teller's wrist. "Please. Call the police. There are three men outside waiting to rob me."

༄

The guard and assistant manager escorted Willie into an office where they waited for the manager, who arrived moments later, his eyes wary, as if suspecting that this might be some elaborate robbery ploy. He took a seat behind a desk and introduced himself even though his name was lettered on a metal nameplate: Walter Hepple.

"Willie LeMat."

"The police are on the way, Mr. LeMat. Can I get you anything? Coffee? Water?"

"Water."

"Rick, will you get Mr. LeMat a bottle of water, please?"

The guard, gnawing his gum with his front teeth, waited a

moment before responding, as if insulted by such a demeaning task. The police arrived, two state troopers of formidable size. Rick returned with Willie's water and was immediately sent out again for more chairs and then directed to return to his post at the door. Disdainfully chopping at his gum with his front teeth, he glared and departed. Willie told his story. As he spoke he began to worry about just how much he should say. Forty thousand in traveller's cheques was surely suspicious. But he'd have to report them stolen if he wanted them replaced. So what was the difference? Unless he claimed he *lost* them? Then maybe the cops wouldn't need to be involved. Or would they? And anyway, here they were. The questions began to spin out of control.

"So there were three of them," the older cop was saying. He'd taken off his hat, filling the room with the smell of sweat and leather. His short blond hair was brushed straight back, his sharp nose bent down at the front as if he'd bumped into a wall, and one of his eyes seemed higher than the other. "Have you ever seen any of them before?"

Willie shook his head and hoped the panic in his eyes did not look as obvious as it felt. *Oh, yes, as a matter of fact I have, they stole my pot.* Which reminded Willie of the pot Juliet had left in the Caddie, which Myron had found, which, along with his cheques, must be with them. "I saw their car. A van. They parked right behind me."

"What kind of van, sir?"

Willie told them exactly what kind, but even as he did he realized that of course, if they found them and the pot, they'd also find the cheques, so there was no use hiding the amount.

"They've got the rest of my cheques." He hesitated as if before a plunge. "About forty thousand dollars worth."

At first the cop did not seem to find that unusual. He made a note in his book and underlined the amount twice, two bold strokes. Then he observed that that was a lot of money.

"I'm doing a bit of travelling."

"Uh huh." He shut his notebook, slotted away his pen and looked at his partner, a red-haired man with a short moustache. "Three people in a grey Econoline van with Canadian plates. Can't be too tough to find."

"I don't want to press charges. I just want my money. I want to get going."

The cop regarded him. The eye that was higher than its pair opened wider, and his eyebrow rose as though re-evaluating everything he'd just heard. He sniffed. He looked again at his partner who sniffed back. A signal? A code? One sniff he's lying, two he's okay? He fit his notebook into his breast pocket and buttoned it. Willie began to stammer out more explanations but the troopers went out the door.

CHAPTER 19

WILLIE VISITED THE AMERICAN EXPRESS office and then Thomas Cook and Bank of America, told his story and filled out papers and then gave them Angela's phone number in Seattle. He found the Caddie right where Steve had left it. The spare key was still under the bumper and he simply got in and drove to Seattle and called Angela, giving her a heavily abridged version of what had happened. At her apartment he described it all again, at which point she cried, not just for the beatings and his loss, but, she confessed, for all the years she'd spent directing her anger at him. Her reaction surprised and touched him. He put his arms around her and she didn't pull away but hugged him tight. She said she'd seen Gabriel — another woman already on his arm. Willie patted her shoulder soothingly and, as he did, spotted a backpack in the corridor by the closet.

"So. You're going down to Buenos Aires to see your mother."

"Nope."

He drew away to get a look at her face but held onto her arms. That *nope* was decidedly different from a plain defeated *no*; it bore about it a certain independence of decision, even optimism. "Back up to Vancouver?"

She grimaced and averted her face at such a suggestion. "Burma. I'm going to see U. Can you drive me to the airport tomorrow?"

❧

There were a few weeks left before the rent ran out on her apartment so he camped on the hardwood floor, the muted sounds of the couple in the room below reaching him as they climaxed each night. He did the rounds and picked up his new cheques and each time he was dutifully informed that the stolen ones had been recovered. He imagined Steve and Co. in custody. Including Lance and his crew, that made six people who'd be hunting Willie. He felt ill with foreboding. What did you get for possession of stolen traveller's cheques and a quarter pound of pot? Thirty days? Three months? A fine? Deportation? He reflected that a public caning would be fun to watch, and considered making enquiries, then let it go for fear of attracting undue suspicion. Either way, he wouldn't be returning to Vancouver any time soon, which presented the question: Now what? Traumatic changes in lifestyle and location awaited. Fly down to Guadalajara and find Carmen? Beg? Plead? He got the number of the Hotel Francés from the international operator and began punching in the numbers, but hung up. Over the next couple of days he did that again and again, working out the Spanish in his mind, *Carmen Conway por favor? Carmen Conway esta ahi? Quiero Senhora Carmen Conway?* But he knew it was too late, and as much as it hurt he knew it was for the best.

Willie phoned Rollo and got the answering machine, didn't know what to say, so hung up. He called again, early and late, and eventually it occurred to him that maybe Rollo had done a back door and hopped a flight to Mexico and met Carmen. He had a vision of Rollo in a mariachi suit and sombrero. They'd probably headed down to the coast to his timeshare in Puerto Vallarta. Willie grew depressed all over again. He could already feel summer flattening out, the prescient leaves drying and the days shortening. He took long walks during which he sought solace in profound conclusions, but all he got were sore feet. Then the rent ran out on the apartment and Willie had to leave because the landlord had a new tenant.

He drove north. Was it possible that Steve and Co. were out already? He'd been scouring the newspaper ever since but had seen no reports. When he reached Blaine he turned east, found Diane's, drove on past and composed himself before turning around and pulling in by an old Ford Galaxie 500. It was afternoon and the scabrous orchard seemed to tremble in the heat. The grass was high and brittle. The place looked deserted. He went up the front steps and knocked and waited and then knocked again. Nothing. Her mailbox was full. He opened it and looked at the name: Diane Booker. He walked around back. He wandered among the trees and found the spot where he and Diane had watched the meteors. Some of the trees had escaped the tent caterpillars and borne fruit. He shook one and apples thudded down and he gathered them up. He returned to the car and dumped the apples onto the passenger seat and then contemplated the house. Apparently she was having a good time down south with Ed. Everyone was somewhere but him. He sat in the car eating the rot-free sections of an apple, the door open, the windows down. He stayed there until the sun dropped and the shadows stretched long upon the ground.

Later, he pulled the car in behind a chestnut tree, out of view of the road, and spent the night on the rear seat. In the morning he washed and drank from a spigot by the back door. He ate more apples and then foraged along the fence for blackberries. He found some late blooming clover and on a whim ate it, too. Back at the house he discovered the remnants of a garden that included parsley, a few shrunken tomatoes and a zucchini. He left them where they were and drove into Blaine to the same Denny's where he'd gone that first night, and was a little disappointed that Lupe was not working. He ate breakfast and drank three cups of coffee and stared out the window at the cars heading north into Canada.

He circled the block three times then parked on the next street over and walked cautiously up the alley. Besides anxiety, an immense feeling of lament filled him. When he reached the carport, he studied the fresh oil-stains like a tracker reading signs. One thing his van had never done was leak oil. Rollo? Lance? Steve? He peered over the carport's half-wall at the house. It looked quiet. The lawn was high and the grass had grown in where Ed's Winnebago had been parked. Willie approached the house with care, studying the windows, glancing around, listening. Surely Lance and his buddies, as with Steve and his crew, would have come and gone by now, cleaned the place out, indulged in whatever malicious handiwork took their fancy then buggered off. He halted at the foot of the stairs, breathless, his heart hammering so hard he feared for his valves, ready to flee at the least flicker.

He winced at each creak of the steps. At the top he peeked past the curtain. Nothing. Everything looked as he'd left it. He tried the door. Locked. Reassured, he dug out his key and slid it in and carefully turned the knob. As he pushed the door open he stepped back, ready to leap down the steps and run, but all that confronted him was an empty kitchen. He stepped in and looked around: the furniture and everything else was there, even the moo-cow milk pitcher, and six empty Pilzn Urquell bottles were on the table. Something touched his shin and he leapt. Boyd. Locked in the entire time, the cat looked crazed. Willie groaned and picked up the frantically purring animal. He could feel the alarming difference in his weight and, as he stroked him under the chin he apologized. He got the bag of Iams from under the kitchen counter, and Boyd had his head in the bowl and was eating even as Willie was pouring the pellets. He stood there for a while, watching the cat eat and only gradually became aware that something was wrong, something was missing: Carmen's self-portraits. The walls were bare. He checked all the rooms and discovered that every picture was gone. He opened the closet: her clothes were gone too. He sat down on the bed, hands dangling between his knees. What had he expected? He didn't know, maybe nothing, maybe exactly this, but it still hurt; what a relief he hadn't flown down to Mexico only to find Carmen in Rollo's arms.

He went downstairs. Tables overturned, pots flung, bulbs shattered, wires frayed. As he wandered among the wreckage, the small clay balls that had filled the pots crunched under his feet. Nothing was worth salvaging. Back upstairs in the living room he discovered that the TV and CD player were also gone.

The late afternoon was slipping into evening and the sunlight was taking on the deeper, richer, deceptively meaningful tones of a more reflective hour. He was tempted to spend the night but was too fearful to sleep after all that had gone on here. He spent the night on the back seat of the Caddie and dreamed of pennies being flattened on railroad tracks until they were so large they drooped like Salvador Dali watches. In the morning he returned to the house, again taking care to circle the block and park a few streets away before coming up the alley. Once inside, he called the international operator and got the number of Diane Booker. She answered on the second ring. She didn't seem surprised to hear from him. "Good timing," she said. "I just got out of a cab from the airport."

Willie plunged ahead with his pre-planned speech. "I wanted to apologize again and make sure things were, you know, all right."

"Actually, I should thank you." He heard a chair scrape the floor like she was sitting down to prepare for a lengthy talk. "I didn't realize how badly I needed to get away."

"So Mexico was good."

"Very good. The orchard wasn't the only thing that was choking." She paused, and, during the two heartbeats of silence, Willie feared it would become uncomfortable, but Diane was talking again, "Juliet found us." There was a playful lilt to her voice.

"Juliet?"

"Caught up with us in Alamos."

"Was Ed happy?"

She laughed loudly, as if that was about the silliest question she'd ever heard. "She had a lot of nice things to say about you." He could hear her smiling as she spoke.

"Well, I'm glad." And he was; he was both flattered and relieved, and a little embarrassed at imagining Juliet and Ed singing his praises.

For a while Willie and Diane talked about her plans for the orchard. She had a lot of work over the winter if she was going to make a go of the place, plus the house needed repairs. She asked if he was going to continue with his career as a farmer.

He looked around the kitchen. He could smell the milk curdling in the pitcher and see a fly trapped in a beer bottle. It buzzed, rested, buzzed again, but it would never get out, not without luck or help. "No, I don't think so." Then he added, "Not that stuff, anyway."

There followed a silence that was indeed awkward.

"Well, if you ever get down across the line again you should pop in."

He weighed her tone. Offhand? Indifferent? A mere politeness? Or was she hopeful; was it an invitation: bring your money on down and we'll see what develops? But even before he could interpret her tone, an invisible hand settled on his shoulder and counselled caution. Maybe he should lie and tell her he'd lost all the money? Gauge her reaction? And then? But he was already exhausted and disheartened with such tactics. "I will."

"Good. I'd like that."

"Okay. Great."

There was a pause, as if she too was weighing the tone of his response. And then her voice, bright, chipper, though perhaps a bit distant, said, "Good," as if she was looking around the room and growing bored, or noticing the tasks awaiting her and was growing anxious to get at them.

"Okay," he said. "I just felt bad about what happened and wanted to be sure, you know, that things were all right."

"I'm okay," she said. "It was probably good that you showed up. No, it was good, definitely good. I needed to get away, I really did. Thank you."

Feeling buoyant, as if he'd inhaled helium, Willie got bold. "Would've been nice to meet up with you. You guys," he added, cursing himself for waffling. "Down in Mexico."

"Yeah," she said, judiciously, weighing it out and agreeing with him. "It would have been fun."

Would have been . . . A woman he'd met one time and it was all in the past tense. But that was just it, a woman he'd met once. "Maybe next time," he said.

"Maybe."

And with that, they hung up at the same time.

He took a last wander around the house and then halted and put his palm to his forehead, appalled at what he'd nearly done. His toolbox. He went back down into the basement and knelt before it as if at an altar. Opening it, he recognized the familiar old smell of steel and wood and oil, and made sure everything was there, his hammers, his Japanese draw saws, his wood-handled screwdrivers, his chisels and planes, his whetstones. Reassured, he closed it and locked the twin hook-latches. On a ledge he discovered an Aspirin bottle full of pot seeds. Leave them? He slipped them into his pocket — that and both pairs of trimming scissors. He found Boyd's cat carrier and went back up to the kitchen. Boyd's food bowl was empty and he was gazing at Willie. Willie got a large bath towel and put it in the carrier, refilled the bowl and put it inside and then pushed the cat in after and locked the grille. On the way out, he again heard the fly buzz in that beer bottle on the table. He picked the bottle up and watched the creature batter itself against the tinted brown glass. He stepped onto the porch and with one gesture, as if throwing a knife, tried ejecting the fly, but it stayed where it was. He tried again. And again. He squinted in at it. "Hey." The fly continued to buzz. Willie turned and rapped the bottle against the stucco siding; it shattered and the fly circled upward and motored away. Everyone was travelling but Willie. He lay the neck of the bottle on the railing and locked the door, picked up the cat carrier and his toolbox and went down the stairs and headed for the Caddie. A beer, a Pilzn Urquell, seemed like a good idea. But not here, not here.